"You're fighting the inevitable, sweetheart,"

Ken said.

"There's nothing inevitable about any of this, and I am not your sweetheart!"

"I suppose it's a matter of perspective. It's how I think of you, but perhaps you haven't quite gotten to that stage yet."

Beth heaved a sigh. "Why are you doing this?"

"Doing what?"

"Chasing after something that just can't be."

"The truth is, Ms. Callahan, I find you perplexing, frustrating, irritating and incredibly attractive."

"Most of those aren't even good traits...."

Dear Reader,

Welcome to Silhouette **Special Edition**...welcome to romance.

In this festive month of December, curl up by the fire with romantic, heartwarming stories from some of your favorite authors!

Our THAT SPECIAL WOMAN! title for December is *For the Baby's Sake* by Christine Rimmer. Andrea McCreary's unborn baby needed a father, and her decision to marry friend Clay Barrett was strictly for the baby's sake. But soon, their marriage would mean much more to them both!

Lisa Jackson's LOVE LETTERS series continues this month with *C Is for Cowboy*. Loner Sloan Redhawk is hot on the trail of his prey—a headstrong, passionate woman he won't soon forget! Also returning to **Special Edition** in December is reader favorite Sherryl Woods with *One Step Away*.

Rounding out this holiday month are *Jake Ryker's Back in Town* by Jennifer Mikels, *Only St. Nick Knew* by Nikki Benjamin and *Abigail and Mistletoe* by Karen Rose Smith.

I hope this holiday season brings you happiness and joy, and that you enjoy this book and the stories to come. Happy holidays from all of us at Silhouette Books!

Sincerely,

Tara Gavin
Senior Editor

Please address questions and book requests to:
Silhouette Reader Service
U.S.: 3010 Walden Ave., P.O. Box 1325, Buffalo, NY 14269
Canadian: P.O. Box 609, Fort Erie, Ont. L2A 5X3

SHERRYL WOODS

ONE STEP AWAY

Silhouette®

SPECIAL EDITION®

Published by Silhouette Books

America's Publisher of Contemporary Romance

SILHOUETTE BOOKS

ISBN 0-373-09927-4

ONE STEP AWAY

Books by Sherryl Woods

SHERRYL WOODS

lives by the ocean, which, she says, provides daily inspiration for the romance in her soul. She further explains that her years as a television critic taught her about steamy plots and humor; her years as a travel editor took her to exotic locations; and her years as a crummy weekend tennis player taught her to stick with what she enjoyed most—writing. "What better way is there," Sherryl asks, "to combine all that experience than by creating romantic stories?" Sherryl loves to hear from readers. You may write her at P.O. Box 490326, Key Biscane, FL 33149. A self-addressed, stamped envelope is appreciated for a reply.

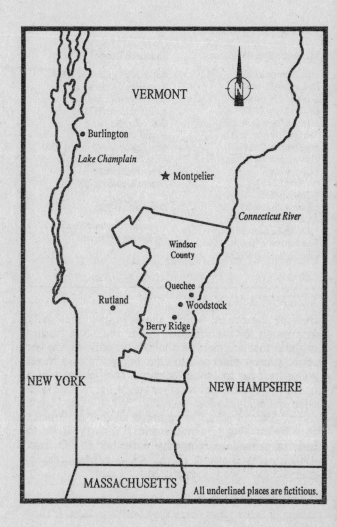

VERMONT

● Burlington

Lake Champlain

★ Montpelier

Connecticut River

Windsor
County

Quechee

Rutland
●

● Woodstock

Berry Ridge
●

NEW YORK

NEW HAMPSHIRE

MASSACHUSETTS

All underlined places are fictitious.

Chapter One

Vermont! In winter! It was the last place a once fanatical California surfer had expected to wind up.

It was also the last place anyone would look for him, Ken Hutchinson decided as he reached for the phone. And that was all that really mattered.

Hesitating, he fingered the business card in his hand. It was printed on some kind of heavy paper that reminded him of fancy wedding invitations. Embossed in gold, no less. Classy. Expensive.

What the hell! He could use a little class in his life. He could certainly afford to pay for it. After more than ten years in professional football and quarterbacking the Washington Redskins to two back-to-back Super Bowls, he had a bank account about a million times bigger than his worried parents had anticipated during all those years when they had wondered if they

would ever get him off the beach long enough to finish high school, much less college.

Thanks to a degree in finance and continuing education classes during the off-season, Ken had determinedly learned how to manage all that money wisely.
He had slowly and methodically assembled an invest-
ment portfolio that paid outrageous dividends. His
financial success had earned him the kind of respect
usually reserved for smart mutual fund managers. He
had even run an off-season financial-planning semi-
nar for his teammates, trying to keep them from falling prey to some of the shady advisers who latched on
to football heroes hoping to cash in on their fame.

More than likely there would never be a chain of
Ken Hutchinson restaurants or Ken Hutchinson auto
dealerships or Ken Hutchinson surf shops, for that
matter. His ego didn't need to see his name flashing in
neon from every street corner. His investments tended
to be carefully discreet, disgustingly sound and, on
those rare occasions when he did take a risk, wildly
lucrative. The only attention he craved these days was
from his broker.

The truth was, he had just about had his fill of no-
toriety. Thanks to a strong arm and quick feet, he had
had the kind of fame many men would envy, along
with enough commercial endorsements to pay for his
seven-year-old daughter's college education, right on
through a Ph.D., if that's what she wanted.

Unfortunately, at the moment Chelsea seemed to be
having difficulty mastering second grade. Lately she'd
become unruly, inattentive and, according to the
nearly hysterical teacher who called him at least once

a week, destined for juvenile hall. Despite that rather dire prognosis, Ken thought she was just about the smartest, spunkiest kid he'd ever met and he was damned lucky to have her.

By most people's standards, he had it made, all right. At least, he had until that second Sunday in August, barely into the exhibition season, when his knee had been shattered by a bone-crunching tackle, pretty much ending his football career. The surgery had been considered a success but at thirty-two, he wasn't masochistic enough to believe that even the most arduous physical therapy could put him back on the field for one or two more outstanding seasons. If he was lucky, he might salvage a year as a starter. Then he'd start the slide to backup and finally he'd be lucky to wind up as third string quarterback on a team going 4 and 12. He had too much pride to set himself up for that. He would have preferred to go out in a blaze of Super Bowl glory one last time, but at least he was leaving in the midst of a winning season with his per-game passing yardage records intact.

He supposed it was somehow fitting that the injury had come only a few weeks after his wife had announced that she wanted out of their ten-year marriage. She had added that she would be flying to some Caribbean island he'd never heard of for a quickie divorce that same afternoon if he would sign the papers she had all ready for him. She had even handed him the pen.

Looking into Pam's cold, blank eyes, he had seen a stranger and suddenly realized that the marriage had really ended long ago. Hell, it probably never should have happened in the first place. She had never wanted to leave Los Angeles and her dream of becoming an actress. For ten years she hadn't let him forget what she had given up to follow him to the east coast.

Recognizing that there was little point in prolonging the inevitable, Ken hadn't seen much reason to fight her, except for Chelsea. He had been adamant about his daughter staying with him. If Pam was going to throw herself wholeheartedly into the Hollywood rat race, she wouldn't have time to give Chelsea the attention she needed. Pam hadn't even bothered to argue. She was too busy planning her long-delayed acting career to worry about the impact her leaving would have on her daughter.

So his days of football glory were over. His marriage was dead. He couldn't bear the thought of going home to California where he would suffocate under all that well-meant parental sympathy. He figured those were valid enough reasons to move to some quiet little backwater town in southeastern Vermont.

With luck, no one there would have ever heard of Ken Hutchinson. Or, if they had, with typical New England discretion, perhaps they would simply leave him the hell alone, anyway. He and Chelsea could both start over. Clean slates and no memories, if such things were possible.

He had visited Berry Ridge, Vermont, a few years back at the invitation of Chester K. Mathias, a blustery, good-hearted sporting goods manufacturer who'd been courting "the decade's greatest quarterback" for a commercial campaign. Ken remembered the town, not all that far from Woodstock, had been isolated and picturesque. At the time, the only activities had been watching wildflowers bloom and long walks. All that peace and quiet, combined with Pam's constant complaints of boredom, had made Ken restless as a caged lion. Now it lured like the aroma of homemade soup on a wintry day.

Despite the fact that that very costly commercial campaign had lost a considerable percentage of its value with the shattering of Ken's knee, Chet Mathias had been the first to call and offer help after the injury.

"You need anything, son, anything at all, you call me," he had said, and Ken had heard the ring of absolute sincerity in the older man's voice.

When Ken had mentioned that he'd wanted to get out of Washington, to settle someplace where he could take a good hard look at his future and his options, Chet had wasted no time in getting the business card for Berry Ridge's best real estate agent to him. Ken studied it again.

According to Chet, Beth Callahan not only handled the finest properties in the Berry Ridge area with brisk efficiency, but she was also willing to coordinate dozens of extra details, the kind of things that left Ken bemused. What did a guy who had spent most of his personal and professional life outdoors know about wallpaper, for example? And he knew more about AstroTurf than he did about carpet.

Pam had tried to get him involved in selecting the decor for their home in a pricey Washington suburb and had finally given up in disgust when he hadn't been able to tell the difference between the dozens of white paint samples she had spread out on the coffee table. Worse, to his wife's way of thinking, he hadn't cared. He seriously doubted he would be any better at it now. Whatever her consulting rates were, Beth Callahan sounded like a godsend.

From Chet's description of her limitless virtues, Ken pictured a mousy, intense, middle-aged woman wearing sturdy shoes and tweed, with bifocals perched on the end of her narrow nose and her fingers permanently affixed to the top of a calculator. He didn't care what she looked like, as long as she could get him settled with a minimum of fuss and maybe teach him to bake chocolate-chip cookies before Chelsea staged a rebellion. At the moment, his culinary skills ran to barbecuing steak on a grill. With a foot or more of early snow on the ground in Vermont last time he'd checked, he'd freeze his buns off unless he developed a more varied cooking repertoire.

Was he making the right decision? he wondered, struck by an unexpected attack of anxiety. For all the interest Pam had shown in her lately, Chelsea had virtually lost her mother. Even so, he wondered if his daughter would be better off in California, where she would at least have her grandparents for emotional support and an occasional whirlwind visit from her mother. Maybe what threatened to be suffocating to him was exactly what Chelsea needed in her life right now. But how the hell was he supposed to know with any certainty?

Suddenly the whole prospect of single parenthood took on daunting proportions. Up until now, he had been mostly an absentee father, at least during training camp and football season. Now he was essentially all his daughter had. There was no counterpoint to his decisions. There was no sharing of responsibility. What if he made a royal mess of things and damaged his daughter irreparably? Was that something this Beth Callahan could fix, as well?

No answers flashed with laser clarity on the opposite wall. No advice hummed through the air. Just like all those Sunday afternoons when he'd had to make a last-second play call at the line of scrimmage, the decision was his. He would either be a heavy or a hero, but the clock was ticking and he had to do something. With a heavy sigh, he picked up the phone and dialed.

For better or worse, it looked as if he were going to Vermont. In winter. Heaven help him!

It was absurd to fall in love with a house, Beth Callahan thought as she stood in front of the Grady place just as she did almost every afternoon, but this house seemed to epitomize her shattered dreams. The big, faded white Victorian with its gingerbread trim practically cried out for the pounding of children's feet across the wide sweep of porch and for the echo of their laughter. A swing hung from a branch of the old maple tree in the front yard. It required all of Beth's resistance and several reminders that she was a professional and a grown-up, not some daredevil kid, to keep her from trudging through the snow for one quick ride in that swing.

She sighed. It wasn't just the swing ride she regretted. It was the fact that she would never live in this house, that she would never fill its five bedrooms with children of her own. Once, that had been her most cherished dream—a marriage, children, happily ever after.

It had almost been within her grasp, too. She had fallen deeply, irrevocably in love with a young widower with two children, a girl and a boy. She had been fascinated with the idea of a ready-made family. In retrospect, she wondered if Peter's biggest attraction hadn't been those two adorable children whose pictures he carried in his wallet.

When Peter Wycroft had finally introduced her to Josh and Stephanie, she had been impressed with their intelligence, charmed by their polite manners and more than ready to be their friend, if not their mother. She had been totally undaunted by all the tales of failed stepfamilies. Hers would not become one of the statistics, not if she had anything to say about it.

Unfortunately, Peter's two children had had other, unspoken ideas about her future as part of the Wycroft family. Both had been about to enter adolescence, both had resented her intrusion into their lives, both had remained determinedly loyal to their mother. And though they were silently sullen in their father's presence, when they were alone with Beth, they had done everything possible to discourage her.

That had been Beth Callahan's first experience with deliberate, malicious animosity. She had been faced with fighting a ghost, a woman whom young memories had rendered perfect. In her dismay, Beth had jumped through hoops trying to win Josh and Stephanie over. Nothing she tried—from kindness to outright bribery—had worked. She hadn't even dented their stubborn resistance. And with each failure, she had lost a little more of her self-confidence.

Everyone had said they would come around eventually. There was practically a textbook timetable for these things, if one survived the stages in between.

Peter had been so certain of that that he had insisted they go ahead with their wedding plans, despite the objections of his children. Beth had been nagged by doubts, but with one last burst of faith, she had dismissed them. She had believed with all her heart that, given time, she could succeed in earning the love of Peter's children. Hadn't everyone always said that Beth Callahan was meant to be a mother? And no two children had ever been in more desperate need of a mother's love.

Beth's faith had suffered its first blow when Stephanie refused to allow Beth to attend parents' night at school along with Peter. It had cracked a little more the first time Josh ran away, blaming her for his not wanting to live at home anymore. It had taken a nosedive when Peter undercut her attempts at discipline time after time.

There had been incident after incident, some small, some large, chipping away at Beth's belief in her own maternal instincts and keeping the household in constant turmoil. For three years she felt as if she were living in an enemy camp with no reprieve in sight. Of all the roles she had ever envisioned for herself, wicked stepmother had never once been among them.

The final blow to the marriage had come when Peter had refused to consider having a child of their own, blaming the tension in the family entirely on Beth. "After all, you're the adult here. If you can't handle two teenagers, how on earth do you expect to deal with an infant?''

His decision, which he had declared irrevocable, had destroyed not only the marriage but the last of Beth's already tattered self-esteem. She had left with little pride and no self-confidence, but had accepted a tidy settlement that had enabled her to move as far away from California as she could get. She had firmly declined alimony, but that lump-sum payment for three years of hell had allowed her time to get her real estate and interior designer's licenses and to open her specialized agency.

Her wildly successful one-woman operation offered everything from the property itself to choosing wallpaper for the client rich enough to customize a country house but unwilling to spend the time and energy it took to do it right. Beth didn't want it to appear that the sale of a client's home hinged on the buyer accepting her additional services, so she optioned her chosen listings herself at a fair market price. She kept only a select few homes on this basis but they were the cream of the market. Each project required patience and dedication, something a good many of the buyers lacked and which Beth had in abundance.

Of all of her select listings in Berry Ridge and the surrounding countryside, the Grady place was Beth's favorite project. She almost hated the prospect of giving it up when it sold. And though she could have afforded to keep the house herself, she had no desire to rattle around in the lonely rooms or to look longingly out the window at an empty swing. She wanted to see the house occupied by the large, happy family it deserved.

Her particular dream for the old Victorian made the call from Ken Hutchinson somewhat disconcerting. He had been referred to her by a satisfied client who had since become a good friend, Chet Mathias, so she knew this Mr. Hutchinson could afford not only her pricey listings, but her additional services, if he wanted them.

But in their brief conversation on the phone yesterday, he had made no mention of a wife, much less children. He'd simply asked what she had available, then picked out three houses based on her detailed descriptions without giving anything away about his own requirements. He had made an appointment to see them all this afternoon, starting with the Grady place.

As a result, Beth had taken an instinctive dislike to him on the phone. He had set her teeth on edge with all of his cool, businesslike questions about plumbing and wiring and heating. The questions were reasonable, but the fact that he'd concentrated on those issues more than any other told her a lot about him. He certainly hadn't sounded like the kind of man who'd bring much liveliness into any house. In fact, he had sounded like a crotchety old bachelor, who had grown more set in his ways with every passing year.

As she waited, shivering just a little in the icy air and watching the sunlight catch on the old rippled glass of the glistening windows, she was almost tempted to break the appointment. Only her pride in her professionalism kept her from doing that. At the very least, though, she would steer Mr. Hutchinson to another property, one that was smaller and more austere, to suit his personality.

Her first clue that she might have misjudged her client was the swirl of powdery snow that rose as an expensive, deep green sports car tore up the lane. The driver was apparently recklessly oblivious to the icy conditions. He was bouncing over the ruts carved by last spring's rains as if they were no more than a minor nuisance. The driver swerved with the skill of an Indy 500 competitor, never once slowing his speed. She had to struggle to reconcile this image of Ken Hutchinson with the stodgier one already formed in her head. It wasn't easy.

But if that was difficult, seeing him emerge from that mud-streaked, highly impractical two-seater was enough to send her into shock. This was not the crotchety, middle-aged man she'd envisioned. If, in fact this was Ken Hutchinson—and she had what she considered to be reasonable doubts about that—he was definitely more hunk than Hitchcock.

Tall and lean, he had a long, purposeful stride that occasionally caused him to wince, as if he'd been recently injured and was still not used to the slowing down that required. His sun-kissed brown hair was a shade too long and beguilingly tousled. As if that weren't intriguing enough, he had the sort of engaging smile that probably left most women speechless. Beth hated to include herself among those ranks. Unfortunately, though, she could barely form a coherent thought.

"Ms. Callahan?" he said.

He spoke in that brusque, no-nonsense tone that had so irritated her over the phone. In person, his crooked smile took the edge off it and the glint of amusement in his gray eyes replaced coolness with warmth. No doubt about it, he was a charmer. Which suddenly raised all sorts of images of wild parties and raucous nightlife in her beloved house.

She just couldn't do it. She couldn't sell the Grady place to this man. He would spoil her vision for it. As costly as it would be, she would keep the place herself before she would let that happen.

Beth drew in a deep breath and prepared to do something she had never, ever done before. She was about to lie through her teeth to a prospective client.

She smiled, hopefully matching his grin in warmth and charm and convincing sincerity. "Mr. Hutchinson, I'm terribly sorry for bringing you all the way out here, especially with the roads such a mess."

Wariness immediately replaced the warmth in his eyes, turning them from glimmering silver to the shade of granite. "Is there some sort of problem?"

"Not a problem exactly. It's just that I've made a dreadful mistake." She drew in a deep breath. "You see, this house isn't available after all."

Chapter Two

Ken studied Beth Callahan's face with its model-perfect cheekbones, wide, innocent green eyes and generous mouth and wondered why the woman was brazenly lying to him. She'd planted herself in the middle of the snow-dusted front walk—right next to the prominent For Sale sign—as if she were an armed guard singlehandedly responsible for the safety and preservation of a national treasure.

From where he stood, her stance wasn't justified. The house looked a little too fussy for his taste and definitely in need of fresh paint. Half the boards on the sagging porch were probably rotted through, as well. Maybe this was her sales technique, he theorized. Tell him the place wasn't available, just so she could get him into a bidding war with some nonexistent would-be buyer. Fat chance.

Still, he was intrigued about what had happened between yesterday afternoon and today to get her to take this house off the market. Surely it hadn't been the sight of him, though now that he thought about it, she had regarded him and his car with a certain aura of dislike. It was not a reaction he was accustomed to. Football heroes—even recently fallen heroes—generally had their pick of the female population, whether they wanted them or not. Oddly, though, there hadn't been the slightest glimmer of recognition in this woman's eyes, just that faint expression of disdain.

He studied Beth Callahan's sturdy, low-heeled brown shoes, her tweed blazer, slim brown skirt and the beige silk blouse with its prissy high neck. Ironically, the outfit was just about what he'd expected.

She, to the contrary, was most definitely not. He wondered why an attractive woman no more than thirty had deliberately gone the fashion route of a spinster librarian. She'd even pulled her rich, chestnut brown hair into a severe style, though it hadn't managed to tame all the curls. A few tendrils had escaped to brush against her cheeks. The flush of color that tinted her face as he continued his slow, deliberately impudent inspection and the wariness in her eyes added to the almost virginal aura about her.

Of course, those pink cheeks and wary eyes might also have been due to the fact that she wasn't used to lying. He supposed that would be a lousy trait for a woman whose career depended on her credibility. He had no doubt at all, though, that she'd suddenly veered away from the truth. The way she was unconsciously twisting her gloves into a knot was a blatant giveaway.

"Sold, huh?" he said finally, watching her closely. Some of the color seemed to drain out of her face.

"Um, not exactly," she said, avoiding his gaze.

Ken held back a grin and barely resisted the urge to murmur "Gotcha!" Instead he nodded soberly and strode up the walk, trying like hell not to favor his injured knee. The brace he was supposed to wear had been giving him fits, so he had left it off. Now, between the long drive and the cold, the damn knee ached like the dickens.

He glanced back and saw that she was still rooted in place. "Come on, Ms. Callahan. Let's get a look at the house. No deal's final until the money's in the bank."

Despite his encouragement, he noticed that the reluctant Ms. Callahan was still lagging behind. With his hand on the doorknob, he beamed at her. "Is there a problem?"

"No," she conceded. "I suppose there's no harm in looking."

As she joined him on the porch, he tested a couple of the boards with his weight. "Rotten," he muttered. Probably termite infested. It was just as he'd expected. The house was a money pit.

Rather than being offended by his remark, she seized on his critical comment as if he'd tossed her a lifeline. In fact, a smile spread across her face. That heart-stopping smile made his blood hum in a way it hadn't for some time now. It was a good thing, too. It was damn cold outside.

Moving a little faster now, she stepped toward a sagging shutter and fingered it pointedly. "You're right, Mr. Hutchinson. It really would take a lot of work to fix this up right. Perhaps we should move on. I think you'll find the other houses more suitable." She glanced quickly toward his leg, then away again. "Besides, there are a lot of steps inside."

Ken bristled at the display of sympathy. She had unwittingly fueled his stubborn determination to see this house. "So?"

She winced at his tone, but faced him bravely. "You might find that troublesome."

"I can handle the damn steps," he retorted irritably. He turned to look her directly in the eye. "Ms. Callahan, you have a reputation as the best real estate agent in the area, am I right?"

She murmured assent, that delightful pink tint back in her cheeks again. Whether it was due to pleasure or embarrassment or the blasted freezing wind, he couldn't be sure.

"Then you wouldn't have told me about this house unless it was something special, right?"

She evaded his gaze. "But it's difficult to tell if a house is right for someone until you've met them."

Bingo! "So you don't think this house and I are well suited?"

To his chagrin, she didn't hesitate. "No." She studied him worriedly. "Sorry. I didn't mean to sound rude. Actually, I have a place in town that would be just right," she said with enthusiasm. "It's small, completely modernized, well-maintained. I'm sure you'd be much happier with that. It would be perfect for entertaining.''

"Ms. Callahan, I don't do a lot of entertaining."

Her spirits deflated as obviously as if he'd poked a pin into a balloon.

"Oh," she said.

"Now, let's just pretend for a moment," he began in the tone he used when telling a story to his daughter, "that you think this house is suitable for me. Cut to the chase. What are its selling points?"

She regarded him with obvious disapproval. "Mr. Hutchinson, buying a house isn't like investing in a stock portfolio. It's not the bottom line that's important. You should have a feeling for a house. It should reach out to you."

That sounded like heresy to him. Ken knew quite a lot about investing in stock portfolios, but he had to admit buying a house was new to him. He'd figured the strategy was the same: buy low and eventually sell high. Judging from the expression on Beth Callahan's face, that wasn't going to work for him today. He was beginning to get a vague inkling of the problem.

"This house reaches out to you, doesn't it?" he said, throwing her own phrasing back at her.

She nodded, suddenly looking younger and more vulnerable. Appealing, in fact. He wondered why she worked so darned hard to hide her physical attributes.

"Ridiculous, isn't it?" she admitted with a self-conscious shrug that he found downright charming.

"And you don't want me to have the house, because you want it for yourself," he suggested, finally understanding her dilemma.

"No. Actually, the house is mine. That is, I bought it for resale. I want to see it sold to the right people," she blurted out, then groaned. "Sorry. I didn't mean any offense."

Ken had to admit he was intrigued by her notion of who the right people would be for this dilapidated monstrosity. He normally didn't like wasting time on fanciful nonsense, but he was in Berry Ridge overnight, anyway, and he had promised Chelsea he'd come home tomorrow with pictures of their new house. He was hoping to spark some enthusiasm for the move she'd been resisting from the minute he'd mentioned the possibility.

"Tell me what you see in the house," he urged. "Room by room."

As she listed its attributes, which were a wide stretch of anybody's imagination as far as he could tell, Ken began to see it through her eyes. He could also begin to imagine Chelsea clattering up and down the stairs, sitting in the window seat upstairs on a rainy day with a book, swinging from the branch of that maple tree—once the worn-out ropes had been replaced—and Chelsea and him baking cookies in the old-fashioned oven, which probably had about another fifteen minutes of life left in it.

"Sold," he said when Beth Callahan had toured him through every room, delivering her sales pitch at last with unchecked enthusiasm. She looked stunned . . . and adorable.

"But..." she began, then apparently lost her tongue.

"What's the asking price?" He kept his gaze pinned on her face to make sure she didn't inflate it outrageously.

"Three hundred..." She met his gaze and blinked, then sighed. "Two hundred and fifty thousand."

"I'll pay two hundred."

It was the first time in his experience he'd ever seen a real estate agent look utterly defeated at getting a firm offer that was clearly above the property's appraised value. He'd checked it out the day before and knew it was worth no more than a hundred and ninety thousand, according to the tax assessor's office.

"Are you sure?" she asked, casting one last wistful look toward the house.

"Absolutely."

She held out her hand. "Then I suppose we have a deal, Mr. Hutchinson. I hope you'll enjoy the house. The papers will be ready as soon as you can arrange financing."

She added the latter with the air of someone clinging to a last desperate hope that he would be disqualified for the mortgage. He dismissed an instant's guilt for robbing her of her treasured house, then announced cheerfully, "That's taken care of. I deposited cash in the bank here this morning. We can take care of all the details first thing tomorrow, if that suits you."

She looked as if she might cry, and suddenly Ken had the oddest desire to pat her consolingly on the back. Or maybe kiss her until she smiled again, which, he decided, was a very bad idea. Still, to be fair, he would give her one last shot to stake her own claim on the house. "Are you sure you don't want to keep this house for yourself?"

"No," she said unconvincingly, her gaze pinned on that swing. "I hope you'll be very happy here. Berry Ridge is a nice community."

She said it in a flat, unemotional tone, as if she thought this sale had just caused the town's property values to plummet, rather than just the opposite.

"Do we *have* to move to Vermont?" Chelsea demanded later that night when Ken called home.

The question had him rubbing his head, which was starting to pound. It seemed nobody today wanted him to buy this house. He held back a sigh. "It's for the best, Shortstuff. You'll love the house. It's like something out of a storybook."

"But, Daddy, I like *this* house. I have friends here. I like *my* school."

"Your report cards aren't much indication of that," he countered dryly.

"I'll do better. I promise. *Please.*"

Even though the tearful plea cut straight through him, Ken kept his own voice firm. "We're moving and that's that."

"But you didn't even discuss it with me," she said in that grown-up way that mimicked her mother.

Forgetting that she was seven, not twenty-seven, he kept the argument alive instead of asserting his authority and putting an end to the debate. "I told you exactly what I had in mind before I left to come up here."

"You *told* me. You didn't *ask* me. That's not a discussion."

"Don't you want to make new friends? You can learn to ski here. There's already snow on the ground."

"I hate snow!"

This from the child who'd practically caught pneumonia the year before when she'd built an entire snow family in their yard, then snuck out of the house after dark in an attempt to spend the night with them.

"You know that's not true," Ken replied, clinging to a last shred of patience. "It's just that this is something new. I know you've already had a lot of changes in the past few months, sweetie, but this one will be for the best. You'll see. Now put your grandmother back on the line."

Pam's mother had pitched right in when her daughter had run off and abandoned them after the divorce. She had come over every day to be there for Chelsea after school, had left dinners for the two of them in the refrigerator and hadn't even hesitated when he had asked her to move in to baby-sit while he made this trip. She was all alone since her husband had died and she enjoyed helping out. Delores Jensen possessed all the calm stability that her daughter had lacked. Ken genuinely loved and respected her.

When she had taken the phone from Chelsea, he asked, "How is she really feeling about this move?"

"It's not the move she's fighting. Not really. It's all of the changes. She'll be fine, once you're settled in up there."

"Are you sure?" he asked, oddly in need of reassurance.

"Ken, you're doing the right thing. A new start will be best for both of you," Delores said firmly.

She muttered a curse he hoped Chelsea wasn't still around to hear.

"Honestly, when I see the disruption my daughter has caused this family, I could just shake her," she said.

"You can't blame Pam for going after what she wants," he soothed with more goodwill than he realized he held toward his ex-wife. "She probably should have done it years ago. Instead, she married me and tried to be satisfied with being a wife and mother. She wanted to be on the big screen, not in some amateur little theater."

Delores sighed. "I suppose you're right. I suppose I can always hope she'll be a better actress than she was a wife."

"Hey, she's bound to be. She fooled me all these years into thinking she was happy."

His ex-mother-in-law chuckled at last, just as he'd intended. "She didn't deserve you, you know."

Ken laughed at that. "The truth of it is, she probably deserved something better. If you believe all the tabloids, I wasn't anybody's idea of a perfect husband, Delores. I just hope I can make up for that by being a decent father."

"You always have been. Nobody who knows you ever believed all that junk the tabloids printed about you being a playboy. You never looked at another woman once you and Pam got married."

"You sound so sure of that," he said, grateful for her faith in him.

"I know you. Now, tell me about the house. Will there be room for me to come visit?"

He laughed. "The place has five bedrooms."

She gasped. "Oh, my! I thought you wanted something small that wouldn't require much upkeep."

"I'm afraid I got caught up in the excitement of the moment."

"Meaning the real estate agent was either beautiful or incredibly persuasive."

"Neither." He thought of Beth Callahan's generous mouth and thick, curly hair. "Not exactly, anyway. She didn't want me to have the house."

"Why on earth not?"

"I think she found me lacking in some way."

Delores Jensen chuckled. "She must have been blind."

"You're prejudiced."

"Hey, I saw that calendar you posed for, remember. I'm not too old to recognize a hunk when I see one."

"I don't think it was my physique that turned her off."

"Then what was the problem?"

Ken recalled the way Beth Callahan had talked about the house, the way her eyes had lit up when she'd described how suitable it was for a large family.

"I think she was hoping for that TV family. You know the one. With John-Boy."

"The Waltons?"

"Yeah," he said with a slow smile. "That's it."

"Doesn't she realize they're just make-believe?"

"I doubt it. Something tells me that Beth Callahan has some very old-fashioned ideas about family."

"I see," Delores said, sounding as if she'd just made an intriguing discovery.

"Forget it," he said hurriedly.

"I didn't say a word."

"You didn't have to. Your reputation as a matchmaker is legendary. Half the bachelors on the team refuse to even meet you since you fixed up Claude Dobbins and practically escorted him all the way to the altar."

She ignored the gibe. "Beth Callahan, huh? I can hardly wait to meet her."

"Don't hold your breath," he muttered to himself.

"I heard that," she said, laughing. "Will we see you tomorrow?"

"I may stay on a couple of days to get the renovations under way. Is that a problem for you?"

"Of course not. You know I love staying with my baby."

"Then I'll call you tomorrow and let you know my exact plans."

"Sure you don't want me to drive Chelsea up?" she teased. "I'd be happy to. Maybe I could give you a little advice on decorating...or anything else that might come up."

"Good night, Delores."

"Is that a no?"

"That is definitely a no."

The very thought of his ex-mother-in-law getting a look at Beth Callahan sent a shudder down his spine. He hadn't been joking about her penchant for matchmaking. What he hadn't said was that she seemed determined to choose the most incongruous people to pair off. Somehow, though, the pairings worked. Right now, he couldn't imagine a more unlikely couple than prissy Ms. Callahan and the reportedly daring, reckless playboy of the Washington Redskins. It would probably be a challenge Delores couldn't resist.

Chapter Three

The next morning Beth was still astonished by her uncharacteristic behavior. She wasn't particularly proud of herself. In fact, she couldn't imagine what had gotten into her. She'd taken one look at Ken Hutchinson, made a judgment about what kind of man he was and completely lost her head. She had not only been downright rude to a man who had done nothing to deserve it, but she had been totally unprofessional in a way that could have destroyed the good reputation she had worked so hard to attain in a tight-knit New England community that wasn't won over easily.

Every time she thought about her actions, she shuddered. Never before had she tried to talk a client out of buying a house. Nor had she ever boosted the price in an ill-considered attempt to block a sale. And all just because she didn't think he deserved to own it. Her license could have been yanked if he had wanted to make an issue out of it.

There was no question that he had known exactly what she was up to. She had been able to read the awareness in his expression. If she were lucky, maybe he would just chalk it off to momentary lunacy. Or, more likely, he would make her pay at some point down the line.

That was probably it, she decided with a sudden flash of insight into the man who had battled wits with her the day before and won. He had struck her as an advocate of the don't-get-mad, get-even school of retribution. That hard glint she had detected in his eyes definitely didn't suggest he would be the type to forgive and forget.

Yet his rare flashes of humor that she had observed were at odds with her overall impression. In many ways, the evidence of a wry wit was even more disconcerting because it had almost tempted her to like him. And in liking him, she would underestimate him, she realized belatedly. It was probably one of his more successful business ploys.

The man apparently also had a streak of stubbornness equal to her own. The harder she had tried to foul up the sale, the more insistent he had become about concluding it. She wondered if he even wanted the blasted house or if he'd just enjoyed sparring with her. She supposed she would know for sure when it was time for the final papers to be signed in—she stole another furtive glance at her watch—about five minutes.

As she sat outside the office of the Berry Ridge bank's president, waiting for her client's arrival, she couldn't help glancing at the time every ten seconds, hoping that Ken Hutchinson wouldn't show up. Maybe even now he was on his way back to wherever he'd come from, having a good laugh at her expense. The humiliation would have been worth it just to keep him out of the Grady place and to keep her from having to face the oddly conflicting feelings she felt in his totally, undeniably masculine presence.

Naturally, however, he strolled through the door right on time. His punctuality grated, even though she knew she ought to be grateful he hadn't kept her waiting, prolonging the uncertainty.

As she took a good long look at him in his tight-fitting jeans, flannel shirt and heavy winter jacket that would have made him a solid candidate to model for the L.L. Bean catalog, her heart thumped unsteadily. She blamed it on disappointment at the now inevitable loss of her favorite house.

The truth was, though, that some seriously deranged part of her found the man attractive, despite the way he'd run roughshod over her the day before. She would hate to be up against him in a cutthroat business negotiation. She had seriously underestimated both his skill and his determination. Under other circumstances, she would have admired those very traits in him. As it was, she floundered unsuccessfully for any logical explanation for the odd, fluttery sensation he caused in the pit of her stomach. Nerves? Maybe. Fascination? All too likely, she decided ruefully.

As Roger Killington, the stuffy, middle-aged president of the Berry Ridge bank, invited them into his office, she tried to gauge his reaction to the area's newest prospective resident. Roger was also president of the Chamber of Commerce and cared a great deal about maintaining the town's upscale serenity. She doubted if that vision included wealthy playboys. Berry Ridge had been gentrified, not turned into some Aspenlike ski resort for the jet set.

To her bemusement, however, Roger was beaming at Ken Hutchinson as if they were old friends.

"The minute you told me yesterday that you were working with Beth, I knew you'd find exactly what you were looking for. She's the best," Roger told him. He beamed at her with almost fatherly pride, which belied some of the battles they'd had about the town's future.

Beth managed a weak smile.

"She does have a way about her," Ken conceded, turning that impudent grin of his on her. His eyes sparked with another display of that humor that warmed her when she least expected it.

Oblivious to the byplay, Roger asked, "So, what did you choose?"

Ken glanced at Beth. "What did you call it? The Grady place?"

Beth nodded.

Roger's expression lit up. "That's terrific. I'm less than a mile away. Maybe we can put together a touch football game in the meadow once the snow melts in the spring. I know half the men in the area will get a big kick out of playing with one of the best. Maybe you could get a few of your teammates up here. We could raise some money for charity."

Roger was so caught up in his plan, he apparently didn't notice Ken Hutchinson's reaction. The man's handsome, chiseled face had turned gray, even though he managed to keep his expression bland. What was going on here? For the first time Beth began to wonder exactly who Ken Hutchinson was.

She didn't have to puzzle over his identity for long. With what was for him an unusual lack of tact, Roger was oblivious to Ken Hutchinson's discomfort. He pulled what looked like a football program out of his desk drawer.

"I knew I had this someplace. Found it at home. Would you mind signing it? My son will be thrilled. He's a huge fan. Hasn't stopped talking about that terrible game back in August." Suddenly he wound down and his voice faltered. An expression of sympathy spread across his face. "Jeez, I'm acting like a jerk. You'd probably like to forget all about that day. How is your knee?"

Although she was hardly a sports fan by anyone's definition, Beth was beginning to piece together the clues. She added what Roger had said to the faint limp she'd detected as she'd watched Ken Hutchinson going through the house the day before. She decided her client must be some sort of football celebrity who was recovering from a serious injury. She glanced into Ken's expressionless face, then met his eyes and realized the torment this conversation was putting him through. Even though she didn't understand the details, she jumped in to try to ease the awkward situation.

"Roger, as you just said yourself, I'm sure Mr. Hutchinson would rather talk about something else," she said firmly. "Perhaps we should get down to business."

Roger looked taken aback by her sharp tone, but his innate diplomacy finally surfaced. "Of course. Sorry." He slid the unsigned program back into his desk drawer. "I have all the papers right here."

Arrangements for the transfer of the title took less time than it took to select a ripe melon this time of year. Beth had to swallow hard as she took the pen in hand to sign the papers. And with her client's steady gaze pinned on her, her signature was disgustingly shaky.

When the deal was closed, it required all of her will to keep the ridiculous resentment she felt out of her voice as she congratulated Ken Hutchinson on his purchase. She drew the keys to the house from her purse and handed them to him.

"I hope you'll be very happy here," she said in a voice so low and unenthusiastic she drew a surprised look from Roger. "If that's all, I'll be on my way."

"Whoa!" Ken Hutchinson said, latching on to her arm with a grip that had probably served him well on a football field. "Trying to run out on me?"

Beth lifted her startled gaze from the hand resting on her arm to his eyes. "Is there a problem?"

"We haven't discussed the renovations. It's my understanding that you can handle those for me. Chet said that was part of any deal you made."

Dear Heaven, this wasn't a twist she'd anticipated. Even as she started to speak, guilt sliced through her. "Really, Mr. Hutchinson..." Catching the warning look in his eyes, the guilt won. She allowed the protest to die on her lips and hoped she could come up with something really good before she was forced to continue to see this man who so unexpectedly and unfortunately stirred her senses.

"Ken," he insisted.

"Mr. Hutchinson," she repeated stubbornly.

His eyes sparkled with mocking laughter as he matched her stubbornness. "Ken."

Beth gave up that fight, saving her energy for trying to make him see reason. "Fine," she said agreeably. "Ken. As for the renovations, I'm sure you have your own ideas about what you'd like to do to the house."

He smiled blandly. "Nope. I don't have a clue."

"But surely..." Her voice faltered.

"I was counting on you."

The look in his eyes threw her. There was nothing innocent about it. Rather, it was warm and very masculine, almost speculative. It took her a minute to gather her thoughts and remind herself sternly that he was interested in her professional skills, nothing more. It still struck her as a bad idea.

"Well, of course, I can recommend local men who are qualified to do anything you'd like with regard to repairs," she offered as a compromise. "As for the interior, I suspect our tastes are very different."

"Afraid I'll want AstroTurf in every room, Ms. Callahan?" he inquired cheerfully.

She could feel the rush of blood into her cheeks. "No, of course not. It's just that—"

"Look, let's cut to the chase," he interrupted with that more familiar brisk tone that didn't make her pulse buck. "I can give you whatever budget you need and carte blanche to make whatever choices you think best."

"I can do anything I want?" she repeated slowly, not quite believing her ears. Temptation rose to crowd out all of her logical arguments.

"Anything," he confirmed.

"Pink marble and lots of velvet?" she suggested, testing him.

He swallowed hard, but nodded. "If you think that's appropriate."

She found herself laughing at the brazen lie. "You must figure you're safe on that score. Choosing pink marble and velvet to decorate a house for someone like you would ruin my reputation forever."

He grinned back at her. "I was counting on that."

"I'm sure you were," she said dryly. "Okay, exactly what do you want me to handle?"

"Everything."

At the prospect of working closely with this man for the weeks, maybe even months it would take to complete renovations on the Grady place, alarm bells went off in her head. Still, it was the opportunity she'd dreamed about to restore the house to the country-style showplace it must have been around the turn of the century. And she'd just about run out of graceful ways to try to turn the job down.

She glanced at Roger and had to smother a laugh at his expression of bemusement. No doubt he couldn't imagine any sensible businesswoman saying no to an opportunity this incredible.

"You realize it could take some time to get everything done. When will you want to move in?"

"As quickly as possible. If you can make a couple of bedrooms livable in the next week or so, the rest can move along at a slower pace."

"Two rooms in a week?" she repeated with disbelief. "That's not possible."

"Sure it is," Roger said hurriedly. "You're a miracle worker, Beth. You know you can get the guys in town to do anything for you."

"For a price."

"Pay the price," Ken said without hesitation. "After experiencing firsthand what a tough negotiator you are..." He allowed his words to hang in the air for one pointed moment before continuing. "You have my complete confidence that you'll get the best possible deals to get the work done in a timely manner."

Given what had transpired the day before, that was quite a statement. It also signaled the catch she'd anticipated. He was willing to forget all about her unprofessionalism. In fact, he intended to turn her questionable tactics to his advantage. Beth sighed. She should have known he would win this round, too.

"How hard can it be?" Ken prodded. "A little paint. A couple of beds to start with. The rest can come later."

The comment showed exactly how little he knew about what the project entailed. Maybe when he saw the price tag for doing it her way, he'd back down and let her off the hook. She could always dream.

Once more, she slid her gaze to Roger's. Damn him, he was watching the two of them with the evident fascination of some paternalistic matchmaker. She could just imagine what he'd have to say about the entire exchange at the next Chamber of Commerce meeting. Roger did love to gossip. With a football hero involved, the story would be too juicy for him to pass up.

"Do we have a deal, Ms. Callahan?" Ken asked.

"Do I have a choice?" she muttered under her breath.

He grinned. "Was that a yes?"

She pulled out her leatherbound notebook and jotted a note on it for the following morning. Then she managed her coolest, most professional smile. "I'll have your estimates for you in the morning. About ten, if that's okay?"

"I'll have a pot of coffee waiting in my suite at the inn."

Beth hesitated. She hadn't counted on a meeting quite that private. She'd been picturing someplace nice and public. Maybe the steps of the town hall. Or the inn's small dining room, at least.

"Is there a problem?" he inquired, that challenging glint back in his eyes.

"No problem at all," she lied blithely. The only problem would be keeping her unexpectedly rampant hormones in check and she hardly intended to share that dilemma with a man who probably took such reactions for granted.

* * *

Back at home, Beth shed her fancy boots and traded her carefully selected, oh-so-professional suit for sweatpants and a stretched out, faded T-shirt from a long-ago visit to Disneyland. She made herself a cup of orange spice tea and settled behind her desk, which she'd placed so she could look out the bay window in her living room.

This house was about a fourth of the size of the Grady place—correction, the *Hutchinson place*—but it suited her well enough. She'd chosen it for the bright, cheerful rooms and the view from this one window. She could see the Green mountains in the distance and the birds up close. She'd hung several bird feeders from the bare branches of the trees and scattered seeds across the snow for the birds each morning, which assured plenty of activity. In the spring there were bluebirds and blue jays, robins and woodpeckers. There were fewer birds now, but they were no less fascinating to watch. Every now and then a couple of ducks wandered up from the iced-over pond to get their share of the bounty. She'd even spotted a white-tailed deer early one morning at the edge of the woods. She'd remained perfectly still for several minutes, awestruck, then sighed as the deer had moved back into cover.

In the spring, which seemed to be later and later in coming, the snow gave way to a profusion of daffodils and tulips. She'd planted more bulbs just last month.

She took a sip of her tea and watched the birds until the morning's disconcerting encounter with Ken

Hutchinson began to fade into perspective. This was a job, she reminded herself. And doing it well would simply add to her already impressive credentials. Besides, she owed Chet Mathias for sending her a client. She didn't want to offend a friend by botching the job.

With that in mind, she decided to take Ken at his word and pull out all the stops. She'd been dreaming about the Grady place from the first time she had set eyes on it. She knew exactly how every room would look if she spared no expense, from the design of the wallpaper to the patterns for the upholstery. Like a child furnishing a beloved dollhouse, Beth had combed antique shops from New York to Maine locating pieces she would buy, if only the right client came along. She'd kept file cards on everything from washstands to brass beds with snapshots attached.

Assembling her price lists and samples took the rest of the day with time out only for a quick sandwich. She spent an hour calling the half dozen men she used regularly for everything from electrical wiring to plumbing and painting, checking on their availability. All were currently on other jobs, but every one of them promised to meet her at the Grady place at seven the next morning to give her price quotes for the needed work. Because she paid on time and well, she didn't even have to mention the bonus she would be willing to pay to get them to squeeze this job into their schedules before the hectic rush of Thanksgiving and Christmas holidays. She was a steady enough employer that they were willing to work miracles for her.

At six-thirty she sat back in her chair with a small sigh of satisfaction. So, she thought, she was going to get to fix the Grady place up exactly as she wanted to.

But she still wouldn't get to live there.

Unless, of course, the glint of interest she'd detected in Ken Hutchinson's eyes on more than one occasion turned into something more.

She dismissed the wildly improbable idea as soon as it arose. A man as attractive and eligible as he was would eventually want marriage and children. She had no intention of trying her luck again with either. She'd failed too miserably the first time around.

After all the heartache, she had finally found a sort of contentment. She intended to hang on to it with everything in her. She was alone, but not lonely. At least, most of the time. And even if there were occasional bouts of middle-of-the-night blues, that was better than asking for the trouble a new relationship would bring.

No, her life was fine just the way it was, she concluded decisively.

Unfortunately, she couldn't help imagining a pair of laughing gray eyes mocking her firm resolution.

Chapter Four

The Berry Ridge Inn had been built in the late seventeen hundreds as a gentleman's farm. The house itself sprawled this way and that, thanks to additions tacked on by the generations of Hopewells who had lived there. Increasing taxes and decreasing family size had forced the most recent generation to turn the house into a cozy inn, known for its blazing fireplaces, early American antiques and excellent gourmet cuisine. The rates were exorbitant, but the service was impeccable. And the view from every window was spectacular: snow-shrouded, pine-topped mountains and a glistening lake that was often dotted with ice skaters.

Ken had taken a suite that included a sitting room, which he'd set up with the laptop computer, printer and facsimile machine that went everywhere with him.

The hour or two he spent checking on his investments by modem was every bit as stimulating for his brain as his rigorous exercise regimen was for his body.

He glanced around the room, his mouth curving into a rueful grin. All of the high-tech equipment looked totally incongruous amid the flowery fabric and the eighteenth-century furniture. Still, there was something almost comforting about sitting back in a wing chair in front of the fire with a glass of brandy at the end of the day, the tools of his trade nearby. He decided to mention to Beth that he would like the office in his new home to resemble the makeshift one he had created in the inn. Otherwise she would probably set him up in some chillingly sterile glass-and-chrome decor suitable for the bachelor she apparently thought he was.

The realization that she had him pegged as a jet-setting, single jock had come to him only last night. Though his single status was true enough, the rest was garbage. He hadn't quite decided yet whether to fill her in on the desire for seclusion that had brought him to Berry Ridge or to allow her to continue spicing up her apparently dull life with her wild imaginings.

Beth Callahan puzzled him. Though she seemed to go out of her way to present herself as a staid New Englander, he'd seen intriguing flashes of temper, wit and vulnerability that belied the image. Maybe this morning's meeting would give him some more insight into what made her tick. The challenge of unraveling the complex puzzle she represented lured him more successfully than provocative clothes or seductive perfume ever could have. It gave him something to look forward to over the coming months of self-imposed isolation, far from friends and family.

She was due any minute with her first set of plans for fixing up the Grady house. He had given her a week to do something with the two bedrooms, hardly expecting her to agree to the impossibly tight timetable. He had done it just to test her, and, to his satisfaction, aside from an almost perfunctory objection, she had barely even blinked. She had just jotted something down in that damnable notebook of hers, topped him by saying she would have plans for the whole renovation ready by this morning, then marched briskly out of the bank to get busy.

In most business associates, Ken would have considered such cooperation and equanimity to be worthy traits. In Beth Callahan, he found them disconcerting, two more pieces of the puzzle. He couldn't help wondering how she had ended up in this small rural community. Was she seeking solace from the past, just as he was?

"A fine woman," Mr. Killington had said to him when she'd gone, his expression shrewd.

"If you say so," Ken had replied, wondering why such a fine, efficient businesswoman managed to get his juices going, when far sexier women had tried and failed in the weeks since the demise of his marriage... and before, for that matter.

Maybe it had something to do with the fact that Beth Callahan was totally oblivious to him as a living, breathing male. In true macho form, that made him want to do something—*anything*—to awaken her responses. Perversely, he wanted to see her unruffled, calm demeanor shattered by an explosive climax. His body stirred as he envisioned stripping away those deplorable, boring clothes of hers to discover the woman beneath. He didn't doubt there was one, because he'd seen the unmistakable evidence of dark, smoldering passion in her eyes whenever he had challenged her in some way. Yes, indeed, Beth Callahan would definitely relieve any boredom that set in once he was settled in Berry Ridge.

He poured himself another cup of coffee and sat back with the *Wall Street Journal*. He'd barely scanned the front page when he heard the sharp tap on his door. Glancing at his watch and confirming it was precisely ten o'clock, he grinned. That was one of Beth Callahan's traits he admired most. She might not like the situation he'd put her in, but she was obviously planning to bravely muster through.

"Come in."

The door opened at once. Again, no hesitation. He smiled to himself. A fascinating, complex woman, no doubt about it.

"Good morning, Mr. Hutchinson," she said briskly, her arms laden with samples, which she allowed to tumble onto the room's sofa.

"Ken," he reminded her as he studied the way she looked in what she no doubt considered her less formal work attire: red wool slacks, a soft winter-white sweater, a navy blazer and a jaunty scarf knotted at her neck. Though the outfit was more intriguingly feminine than that unfortunate tweed he'd seen her in before, he still longed to see her in satin and lace with her hair tumbling free of that ridiculously prim knot she'd twisted it into.

To his amusement she barely noticed what he'd said or the way he was studying her. Totally absorbed in her own agenda, she shed her coat and pulled her notebook from her crammed-full leather attaché case. Perching on the edge of the chair opposite him, she tapped a pen against some notation in her notebook.

"Now, then, I have met with the workmen, gone over my figures, and I think we can do this for about ten thousand dollars, except for furniture. I wasn't sure what you might already have." She finally glanced up at him, her expression expectant.

"I'm bringing nothing with me," he said. "This is a fresh start."

She didn't bat an eye. "I see. Did you have an amount in mind for the furnishings?"

He shrugged. "Whatever it takes."

Her gaze narrowed. "Could you be more specific? I don't want to send you into backruptcy."

"There's not much chance of that," he said dryly. "Unless you're planning on solid gold fixtures and rare art for every room."

Serious green eyes blinked at him. "Mr. Hutchinson, perhaps it would help if I knew a little more about you."

He grinned. "You want to know just how rich I am?"

"I want to know something about you," she corrected. "Your likes. Your dislikes. That sort of thing. I gathered yesterday that you play football."

Ken's ego had an instant's pause at the realization that she didn't have a clue who he was. Then he decided that was all to the good. She wouldn't waste much time pitying him. And she obviously wouldn't be catering to him because of his celebrity. A rare sense of calm stole over him at the realization that with Beth Callahan, he could be whatever he chose.

"I used to play football," he corrected. "My career ended in August."

"I'm sorry."

With a sudden lack of bitterness that surprised him, he shrugged. "It happens. I had a great career. How many people can reach the top of their profession by the time they're thirty-two? What about you?"

She looked disconcerted by the question. "I love what I do."

"It shows."

"Oh?"

"Your face glows whenever you talk about your houses."

"You'll probably think I'm nuts, but they're a lot like people," she confided with an oddly wistful expression. "They each have a distinct personality."

The admission didn't surprise him, but it did make him wonder if she had more feeling for these projects of hers than she did for actual people and why that would be so.

"And what about Mr. Callahan? Does he share your affection for real estate?"

"There is no Mr. Callahan."

"Ah," he said knowingly.

She frowned at that. "I was married," she said. "It didn't work out."

She said it with a note that might have been defiance or raw pain. Maybe some combination of the two. At any rate, he flinched at the tone that conveyed far more than her actual words.

"Sorry," he said automatically, though some part of him appeared to be rejoicing at the news that Beth Callahan was available.

"If it hadn't happened, I wouldn't be doing this," she said with a more cheerful air.

"I guess the saying is true, then. Every cloud does have a silver lining."

She grinned suddenly. "You just have to be careful you don't get soaked while you're waiting for it."

Ken chuckled, as much at the unexpected wit as at her determined show of bravado. Obviously there were even more layers to Beth Callahan's personality than he'd initially guessed. It was definitely a toss-up whether it would be more fun to peel them away or to strip her down to the fashion basics to see if she wore serviceable cotton or delicate, sexy lace.

"Mr. Hutchinson? *Ken?*"

Her voice finally cut through the pleasant fantasy he'd been having about her. He regarded her guiltily. "Sorry. I just remembered a call I should have made this morning," he improvised.

"Do you need to take care of it now? I can wait. I'd really like your full attention when we go over this."

He moved his chair a little closer. "Now is fine. And I can assure you that you have my undivided attention."

Apparently something in his voice alerted her that his attention just might not be all business. She shot him a puzzled frown. He grinned and leaned back. "Bring on the samples."

Ken was prepared to be bored to tears, just as he had been when his ex-wife had laid out all those look-alike paint chips. Instead, though, he soon found himself caught up in Beth's enthusiasm. He also began to appreciate the subtle differences in fabric texture and color, especially when he considered whether Beth Callahan's skin would feel like the silk she was proposing to use for a fancy window treatment and whether the shade of material she'd chosen for his office furniture was any deeper or richer than the color of her hair.

In fact, he was gazing intently at her hair when she cut into his thoughts again.

"You're not paying attention," she accused.

"Oh, but I am," he disagreed, and rattled off the costs she'd quoted for various alternatives. "I like this shade of brown for your hair, but not for my office. Your hair catches the light. The fabric doesn't. It's dull and lifeless."

Her startled gaze shot to his. Her fingers lifted automatically to smooth a stray tendril into place. "My hair? What does my hair have to do with anything?"

"Just a color comparison to prove I was paying attention."

She seemed more than ready to accept that innocuous explanation. "What about the gray then? It's very businesslike, especially if we throw in some teal accents."

He shook his head and gestured around them. "I like this."

She took in the flower-patterned upholstery of the sofa and the wing chair in its complimentary solid blue fabric. "This?" she repeated doubtfully. "Flowers? Wedgwood blue?"

"It feels . . . comfortable. Homey. Don't you think so?"

Her expression brightened. "Yes, of course. It's just that I thought for your office you'd want something more . . ."

"Businesslike?" he offered.

"Masculine," she said.

"This isn't clothes. I don't expect the room to make the man. I want a room that's cheerful, that anyone, male or female, would feel comfortable in."

"No game room with pool table and felt-topped card tables?"

"You sound disappointed. Do you play poker or pool?"

She grinned. "Afraid not."

"Do most of my neighbors?"

"I have no idea."

"Then I guess there's not going to be much call for them. For the moment, I just want to get the repairs done, get a couple of beds in and then we can decide what's to be done with everything else." He extracted the estimates she'd drawn up from the pile of papers and samples that had accumulated. He made a few calculations of his own and decided the deals she'd managed to pull together in barely twenty-four hours were more than satisfactory.

"How soon can they get started on this?"

"They promised to get a crew together as soon as I give them an okay."

"Do it."

"Just like that?"

"Are these figures going to change if we debate them?"

"Probably not, although I suppose there's always room for a little negotiation."

"Beth, one thing you should know about me. I know exactly what I want in life and I go after it." He fastened his gaze on her and saw the color rise in her cheeks. "Also, I don't waste time trying to nickel and dime a man who's just trying to make a living. These look like fair prices to me. I see no need to haggle over them. And I want to get moved into this house as quickly as possible. Do whatever it takes to make that happen."

"Will you . . . ?" She swallowed hard. "Will you be moving in alone?"

He was amused by her apparent embarrassment. "No," he said, and left it at that. He could be just as closemouthed about his personal life as she was about hers. He wondered if the flicker of reaction he'd caught in her eyes was dismay.

"Well, then," she said, all brisk efficiency again. "I'd best get busy. I'll call the workmen as soon as I get back home and make arrangements for them to get started."

"Do it now," he said. "And then we can have some lunch."

She stopped in the midst of trying to stuff all her papers back into her attaché case. "Lunch?" she repeated as blankly as if she'd never heard of the meal.

"Lunch. Maybe some clam chowder. A salad. A veal chop. Whatever you like. The food is excellent here." He deliberately dropped his voice to a seductive whisper. "And I understand the chocolate mousse is downright decadent."

She ran her tongue across her lips, as if they'd suddenly gone dry. Ken watched that delicate movement and felt his heart buck. Damn! What was it about this woman's every movement and gesture that got to him? He hadn't stopped thinking about sex and seduction since the moment he'd met her. The irony was that he'd never known any woman more determined not to stir lascivious thoughts in someone of the opposite gender.

"You said you wanted to get to know me," he reminded her. "To help you choose the furnishings. Here's your chance. I'll have to go back to Washington first thing in the morning. It may be a few days before I get back up here."

He made the lunch sound as businesslike as possible. He figured once they were settled comfortably in front of the fire with a glass of wine or two, he could twist the conversation away from himself and toward Beth Callahan. Instinct had made him entrust his home to her. Now, like the rational businessman he was purported to be, he wanted the facts to justify his actions.

Or so he told himself. The truth was, he just wasn't ready to say goodbye to the first woman in a decade who didn't seem to give a damn that he was a football hero. Maybe, just maybe, Beth Callahan would see the real man.

And maybe, by looking into her eyes, he'd begin to figure out who he really was now that the phrase "record-setting quarterback" would no longer automatically be said along with any mention of his name.

At some point between the clam chowder and the chocolate mousse, Beth began to relax and enjoy herself. As she sipped a cup of cappuccino while Ken took a call from a business associate, she found herself leaning back and studying him with more objectivity than she had in the past.

This entire meeting had surprised her. She had known from the first that he was intelligent and shrewd. She had even recognized his quirky sense of humor. What she had failed to see was that Ken Hutchinson was not the arrogant, egotistical man she had built him up to be. Even though he hadn't hesitated to disagree with her, he had been consistently respectful of her opinions. She had expected him to be condescending to her or, worse, to overrule her at every turn, simply because she was a woman or because it was his money they were spending. Instead he had treated her as an equal, as a professional, she admitted with a sense of amazement.

Not that he hadn't noticed her as a woman. She had caught his speculative surveys, the occasional lingering looks that would have turned her insides to complete mush if she hadn't hurriedly looked away. There was enough electricity humming through the air to provide power for his new house through the entire icy Vermont winter. And on some level she couldn't afford to indulge, she was enjoying it, even if his enigmatic response about moving into the new house with a companion had disconcerted her more than she cared to admit.

Suddenly she felt the sensation of his gaze on her again. She glanced up and caught him grinning.

"What were you thinking about?" he asked.

"Plumbing," she said, grasping at the first thing that came to mind.

He regarded her with obvious amusement. "Remind me to check out the plumber, if he can put a glow like that in your cheeks."

Beth almost laughed as she considered his reaction to the portly Chuck Wilson, whose pants tended to scoot dangerously low as the day wore on. She doubted if the grandfather of ten was anybody's idea of a sex object, except perhaps Mrs. Wilson. At any rate, he was hardly in Ken Hutchinson's league and Ken would know that at first glance.

"Worried about the competition?" she asked without thinking, then wanted to die right where she sat.

"What if I am?"

The tone of the inquiry was bland enough, but the implication was very dangerous, especially coming from a man who might very well be committed to someone else. Beth tried to still her suddenly erratic pulse. "We have a business relationship, Mr. Hutchinson. Nothing more," she said, then added emphatically, "Not now. Not ever."

"The plumber's that fantastic?" he said, his gray eyes skeptical.

"The plumber has nothing to do with it," she said briskly. She stood and began gathering her things.

"Don't run off just when things are getting interesting," he taunted.

"You're not my only client," she informed him.

Judging from his expression, he clearly didn't believe that was the reason for her hurried departure. Still he didn't argue as he walked her to the door. She thought she'd made a clean getaway when he said quietly from the doorway, "Just remember one thing, Beth Callahan."

Swallowing hard at the quiet command in his voice, she turned back. "What's that?"

"I may not be your only client, but from this moment on I'm the only one who counts."

She opened her mouth to argue, then snapped it shut as the door was closed softly right in her face. It was probably just as well, she thought even as she fumed. With the money he was currently proposing to spend, Ken Hutchinson really was the only client who mattered. And despite that gauntlet she'd thrown down as she'd exited his suite, the truth of it was, he was the *only* client she had.

She warned herself that she would be very wise to change that situation in a hurry or she would find herself hip deep in the kind of trouble she'd been trying to avoid ever since her disastrous marriage. Right now, it was just a darn good thing Ken Hutchinson was leaving town for a couple of days so she could reclaim her equilibrium and muster her previously well-honed defenses.

If she had any doubts about the need to get a grip on her emotions in a hurry, his admission that he wasn't moving into the new house alone ought to be enough to convince her to keep her distance. The very last thing she needed in her life was a flirtation with a man who obviously didn't take commitment of any kind very seriously.

Chapter Five

"I hear you just sold the Grady place to a man who is drop-dead gorgeous and rich as that king with all the gold. What was his name?" Gillie Townsend said to Beth the following morning, right when Beth was doing her best to put the man out of her mind.

"Croesus," Beth supplied, since she had no intention of discussing the other man.

"Yeah, right," said the thirty-year-old mother of two seated across from Beth in Berry Ridge's one and only coffee shop, which doubled as the town's bakery. The scent of bacon and eggs vied with freshly baked pastries and pies and the aroma of freshly perked coffee.

Gillie propped her chin on her hand. With her blond hair caught up in a ponytail, she looked about half her age.

"So, tell me everything," she insisted.

Beth scowled at her. "Have you and Daniel been married so long that you need to live vicariously through me? If that's your plan, you're going to have a very dull time."

"Obviously you don't understand just how tedious laundry, dirty dishes and conversation with a couple of pint-size hellions can get. Your life is definitely exciting by comparison. I'll bet you've even eaten a meal out that didn't come in a bag."

Beth recalled the clam chowder, chocolate mousse and conversation she'd indulged in the previous afternoon. Apparently something in her expression gave her away.

"You have, haven't you?" Gillie said triumphantly. "I knew it. Did he ask you out to dinner? Where? I'll bet it was at the inn. I heard that's where he was staying, in a suite, no less. What did you have? What did you talk about?"

Beth chuckled despite herself at her friend's enthusiasm. It was definitely time for Gillie to go back to work. Being room mother for her second grader's classroom was not nearly challenge enough for a woman who had once handled mega-bucks advertising accounts in New York.

"It was lunch, not dinner," she told Gillie. "Yes, it was at the inn. We both had the clam chowder. And mostly we talked about fabric samples and plumbing."

"You didn't talk about him? Didn't you find out anything? Is he married? When are you seeing him again?"

"I don't know if he's married, but someone is moving into the house with him."

"A woman?"

"He didn't say. If it is, she's apparently moving into a separate bedroom," she said, suddenly recalling the request of *beds,* plural not singular. She couldn't ignore the relief that suddenly spread through her. "As for the rest, I don't know when I'm seeing him again. He said he'd be back in a few days."

Gillie shot her a disapproving frown. "How could you not find out if he's married, for heaven's sake? What's wrong with you? Was he wearing a ring?"

"I didn't notice," she lied. Actually, she had. He wasn't. She didn't intend to tell Gillie that, though. It would only fuel this absurd fantasy she was hell-bent on inventing. Besides, a lot of married men didn't wear rings. The lack of one was an indicator of status, not a guarantee.

Gillie sighed. "Okay, let's back up. What's his name?"

"Since you obviously possess the detecting skills of Nancy Drew, I'm surprised you haven't found that out already."

"Paula Redding, who heard about him from Denise Winston, who saw him with you when she was driving by the Grady place, said she didn't know any details except that he was built to die for and he drives an outrageously expensive, very classy emerald green sports car. So, give. What do you know?"

"He's some kind of ex-jock. A football player."

Gillie's eyes lit up. "No kidding. What's his name?"

Beth told her.

Her expression turned incredulous. "Ohmigosh," she whispered. "You're kidding? Wow! Wait till I tell Daniel. Ken Hutchinson! Drop-dead gorgeous doesn't begin to describe him."

"You know who he is?" Beth said, then remembered that Gillie and Daniel drove to Boston for football games practically every single weekend of the season. Of course she would know who Ken Hutchinson was. "Tell me about him."

"He's only the greatest quarterback to hit the National Football League this decade! Or he was," she said, her expression filled with sympathy. "He was injured during the pre-season. They say he'll never play again."

So, Beth thought, he had been telling the truth about that. No wonder he'd looked so pained by Roger's tireless goings-on about football. No wonder he'd seemed a bit startled when she hadn't recognized him. He was probably far more used to Roger's behavior than hers.

Gillie regarded her with amazement. "You mean, you really didn't know who he was?"

Beth shrugged. "I didn't have a clue. I don't watch football. He was really great?"

"The best. Not only that, from what I've read, he's really a nice guy. Does a lot of stuff for charity. Of course, he also has a reputation as quite a playboy, according to the tabloids, but who believes them?"

Beth could imagine that there might have been at least the tiniest little kernel of truth in the reports. He'd wasted no time in engaging in a mild flirtation with her. She sensed it had come to him as automatically as breathing, something he probably couldn't quit if he tried.

Gillie apparently regarded her continued silence with suspicion. "You did notice he was gorgeous, didn't you?"

"I noticed," she admitted under that penetrating gaze.

"Good. I guess there's hope for you yet."

"I am not looking for a relationship," Beth reminded her for probably the hundredth time since they'd started getting together for coffee at least once a week. "Been there. Done that."

Gillie waved off the protest. "There are some forces in nature that are just too powerful to fight."

A few days ago Beth would have argued vehemently with her about that. Then she'd met Ken Hutchinson. Now, no matter what she said aloud, she wasn't nearly as certain of anything as she had been. Okay, so maybe there was a wildly passionate fling in her future. She could go along with that. But more? Not a chance.

She looked Gillie straight in the eye. "Ken Hutchinson and I have a business relationship and nothing more."

"Sure," her friend said agreeably.

She didn't look any more convinced than Ken had when Beth had said those same words to him. Beth wondered if either of them realized how irritating their reactions were.

Ken spread the pictures he'd taken of the new house on the dining room table for the benefit of his daughter and his ex-mother-in-law. Delores, he had to admit, was more enthusiastic than Chelsea.

"I love it!" she said at once. "It has fantastic possibilities." She glanced at her granddaughter. "Look, Chelsea, it already has a swing in the yard."

"It's a dumb swing. Besides, I have a whole swing set here," she said, her lower lip set mutinously. She glared at her father. "With a slide!"

"You can have the exact same set there, if that's what you want," Ken said, feeling absolutely helpless. He was convinced this move was best for both of them, but his daughter was hell-bent on making it difficult. She'd been glowering at him from the minute he'd walked in the door. He was trying his damnedest to be patient with her, but it was getting more difficult by the minute.

"I want to stay here with Grandma," she said. "You go live in that awful place."

"Sorry, Shortstuff," he said mildly. "That's not an option."

Tears welled up in his daughter's eyes. "I won't go. I *won't*," she screamed at him and ran from the room.

Ken sighed. He looked into his ex-mother-in-law's sympathetic eyes.

"This won't last," she promised him. "She's just scared."

"What the hell do I do in the meantime? I don't want her to be miserable."

"Get her involved. Let her choose the things for her room. Let her help to make it her house, too." She picked up the snapshots of the bedrooms. "Let her choose which room she wants. Take her to a furniture store to find the right bed, ask her about colors and curtains.''

''I thought that's what I was paying Beth Callahan to do.''

Delores smiled at him. ''I'm sure she won't be distraught if you take one room off her hands. Besides, whose feelings matter more? Chelsea's or the decorator's?'' She studied him intently. ''Or is she already becoming important to you, too?''

''Don't be ridiculous,'' he muttered. ''I barely know the woman.''

''When are you going back up there to supervise the work?''

''I was going tomorrow, but I suppose I'll wait until the day after so I can spend the day shopping with Chelsea tomorrow.''

A triumphant expression spread across Delores's face. ''So you are interested.''

He regarded her irritably. ''I didn't say that.''

She patted his hand consolingly. ''You didn't have to. The fact that you're rushing back up there says volumes. If you weren't interested, you'd wait and go back when the job is finished.''

''She's spending a fortune of my money,'' he countered reasonably. ''Are you suggesting there's something unusual about my wanting to oversee the work?''

''How many shares of that electronics stock do you own?''

He scowled at her. ''Quite a few. What's your point?''

"When was the last time you felt a need to visit the factory?"

"It's not the same thing."

She grinned happily. "Close enough," she said as she headed for the kitchen. She stopped long enough to wink at him. "I can't wait to meet her."

"Don't hold your breath," he muttered in the direction of the closing door.

"I heard that," she called back cheerfully.

Before he could think of anything to counter her convictions about his interest in Beth Callahan, the phone rang.

"Yeah?" he growled.

"Hey, buddy, you okay?" Claude Dobbins asked worriedly. "You didn't go and break something else on that ice up in Vermont, did you?"

"No, you just caught me at a bad time. I was considering strangling my ex-mother-in-law." He figured Dobbins, an all-pro offensive lineman who'd been the target of Delores's matchmaking efforts himself, would understand.

"You touch a hair on that sweet woman's head and I'll personally break your other knee," the three-hundred-pound man said.

"Since when did you start taking her side?"

"Since I realized that marrying Harriet was about the smartest thing I ever did and it wouldn't have happened if Delores hadn't given me a shove."

"I don't recall your having the same attitude when we were trying to get you into your tux before the wedding. Making a fast getaway to Tahiti was mentioned more than once."

"I've wised up since then." He fell silent and Ken could hear him taking a deep breath. "Besides," he blurted out, "Harriet and me, we're gonna have a baby. That's what I called to tell you."

Ken felt the unexpected sting of tears in his eyes. Though Claude had claimed to disdain marriage and everything associated with it, he'd spent his off-the-field free time working with half a dozen children's charities. He was a natural with the kids, sick or well, rich or poor. "Hey, man, that's just about the best news I've ever heard."

"Good enough that you'll be the baby's godfather?" he asked, an oddly hesitant note in his voice.

"You name the time and place."

"Thanks," he said, his relief evident. "We couldn't think of anyone we'd rather have. Think Delores would be godmother? Harriet's got her heart set on it."

"She's right here. I'll let you ask her yourself. When's the baby due?"

"Next May."

"Smart move. It won't interfere with the football season. That'll keep the coach happy. He won't have to fine you for missing a game to be in the delivery room with Harriet. Let me get Delores, so you can tell her."

"Wait one sec, buddy. What's this I hear about you buying a house *and* finding a new lady in Vermont?"

Ken groaned. "I'm going to strangle my ex-mother-in-law, after all."

"No house or no lady?"

"There is a house. Plenty of room for the soon-to-be-enlarged Dobbins family to visit. As for a lady, Chet Mathias introduced me to a woman who is going to handle all the renovations and the decorating. That's it."

A sudden vision of Beth Callahan flashed through his head. His pulse automatically kicked into overdrive. The reaction made his voice less emphatic when he added, "Don't go listening to everything Delores says. The woman has a wild imagination. It comes from those romance novels she reads all day."

"I heard that," the woman in question hollered from the kitchen.

Dobbins was chuckling in his ear. "Oh, brother, I can't wait to see how this scene plays out. I'm gonna get me a front row seat and laugh my head off, just like you did to me."

"Go to—"

"Tsk-tsk. You shouldn't let a little innocent teasing get to you. Isn't that what you were always telling me? Now let me talk to the finest woman in the western hemisphere."

"Only if you promise you won't start conspiring against me."

"The only promise I ever made was to keep the defensive tackles from nailing your sorry butt on a football field," Claude informed him. "And if I hadn't been sidelined for that one damned play back in August, you'd still be the best quarterback in the NFL. I'm never going to forgive myself for that."

Ken had heard the self-accusations long enough. "Stop it. They dislocated your shoulder, for God's sake. It's the only play you've missed in the entire ten years we were together."

"And just look what happened," he said miserably.

"Claude Dobbins, if you don't knock it off, I'm going to start praying that Harriet has quadruplets. You won't sleep from May right on through next season's Super Bowl."

"Look, man, I know you don't blame me, but you can't deny that if I'd been in there, things would have been different."

"Maybe. Maybe not. There's no point speculating. Believe it or not, I'm okay with this. It's not the way I would have chosen to end my career, but it sure as hell beats spending an entire season getting intercepted or sacked on every other play and winding up fired." He glanced up gratefully as Delores came back into the room. "Now, here's my ex-mother-in-law."

She shot him a puzzled look, but accepted the phone.

While she talked to Dobbins, Ken drew in a deep breath and tried to put aside all the memories his friend had stirred up. He picked up the photos from the new house and headed for Chelsea's room. The important thing now was to think of the future. For both of them.

Despite the teasing of his ex-mother-in-law and his best friend, Ken headed back to Vermont two days later. To his astonishment, he was suddenly looking forward to studying wallpaper samples and choosing paint. Maybe he'd go completely off the deep end and do some of the remodeling himself, especially if Beth Callahan would pitch in and work by his side.

He tried not to let himself worry too much about Chelsea's uncharacteristically stubborn behavior. She had professed no interest in looking at furniture for her room or in selecting a color scheme. She wouldn't even go to the store to look at swing sets. Her teacher had called again yesterday afternoon and asked if there was anything going on at home that might explain why she'd gotten into a fight on the playground and another in the lunchroom. Despite the fact that he was uncomfortable with airing his problems to anyone other than family, he had to tell the woman about the impending move. He couldn't say for certain, but he was almost sure he'd heard her utter a sigh of relief. He'd left for Vermont feeling frustrated and angry and uncertain.

Delores had suggested grounding the seven-year-old for her rotten behavior, but he hadn't been able to bring himself to do it. He'd kissed her goodbye this morning and tried desperately not to notice the accusing expression in her big gray eyes.

When she'd shouted after him, "I hate you. I want to go live with Mommy," Ken had thought his heart would break. If he had thought for an instant that letting her live with his ex-wife would put things right, he would have let her go.

But Ken knew better than anyone that Pam didn't want their daughter in Hollywood with her. Because of that knowledge and the terrible guilt it stirred in him, he vowed to make allowances for Chelsea's behavior. She would get over it soon enough and be back to her sunny, normal self. He hoped.

He was still worrying about his daughter when he drove down the deeply rutted lane to his new house. This time he'd come in his four-wheel-drive wagon, a far more practical vehicle for these roads than his sports car. He figured he might as well get it to Vermont. He'd bring the sports car later. Maybe the different car explained why Beth didn't spot him at first. Because she was totally absorbed in her conversation with the roofer, he had time to study her and try to analyze why she, of all the women he'd met, made his heart thump unsteadily.

She was wearing the snug-fitting jeans he'd hoped to catch her in one day. They curved over an enticing bottom and slim hips, then smoothed over perfect thighs before being tucked inside high, sturdy boots. A bulky, fur-lined jacket disguised the shape of her torso, but Ken found he remembered it well enough just from the hints he'd gotten from the fit of that soft sweater and tailored blazer she'd worn the last time he'd seen her.

The collar of her coat was turned up around her ears and a knit cap was pulled down to meet it, leaving only stray tendrils of brown to curve against her glowing cheeks. Even from where he sat observing her, he found it amazing that her hair could catch the sunlight and shatter into so many different shades from sparkling gold to radiant red, all deepened by the basic brown.

She blew on her bare hands to keep them warm as she talked. It was so cold, her breath was visible. He suddenly had the strangest urge to march across the yard and snatch her gloves from her pockets and insist she wear them. Or, perhaps, to just take those frigid hands in his own until they were warm again. He couldn't help wondering if they'd be soft or if there would be calluses from the work she pitched in to do.

Where had this crazy attraction come from? he wondered yet again. He wasn't sure whether he was drawn to her physically, whether he was attracted by her competence, or whether he was intrigued by the vague hints of vulnerability she so rarely allowed to show. It would be easy to dismiss it as simple, straightforward lust, but the truth was, she'd engaged his mind almost as quickly as she'd taunted his hormones. Too few women had ever done that.

Given the flurry of activity inside and outside the house, Ken was suddenly oddly hesitant about intruding. Beth looked thoroughly at home amid the chaos and the workmen. He felt as if he'd suddenly grown an extra pair of hands as he stood awkward and uncertain beside his car. He told himself he might have left, satisfied that there was progress being made, but just then she spotted him and made leaving impossible.

"Hi, there! I didn't expect to see you back here so soon." Her boots crunched over the ice-topped layer of snow as she walked over to join him.

"I told you I'd only be gone a few days. Come here and get in the car where it's still warm. You look frozen."

She laughed. "I'm used to this. It'll have to drop another thirty degrees before it really bothers me."

"It's already below freezing."

"It'll get colder. Trust me."

Ken shivered. "I'll never get used to it. I think I still have California blood."

"You're from California?" she said with a look of surprise.

"Los Angeles."

"That's amazing."

He grinned. "Not so amazing. It's a big city. And since the earthquake, lots of people are *from* there."

"You don't understand. That's where I'm from, too. I've only been living here a couple of years now."

Ken suddenly felt yet another invisible thread tying them together in a way he couldn't explain. "I guess that means we should have dinner tonight and talk about old times."

A sudden wariness flashed in her eyes. "I can't do dinner tonight."

"Can't or won't?"

"Not used to being turned down, are you?"

"Not for long," he said mildly. "Okay, you don't have to say which it is, can't or won't, as long as you agree to breakfast tomorrow instead."

"Sure," she said readily. "Seven o'clock?"

Ken couldn't remember the last time he'd been awake at seven, much less functional. "Seven?" he repeated doubtfully.

She grinned. "You wouldn't want me to report late for work, would you? The crew here starts at eight."

"I admire your dedication, but couldn't you be late, just this once?"

"What kind of example would that set?" she chided.

He sighed. "Seven o'clock. Just don't expect me to be coherent."

"Don't worry, Mr. Hutchinson. I don't expect much from most men." She glanced toward the crew she had working. "Unless, of course, I'm paying them to do a job."

Ken watched her stroll back into the fray with an increasingly familiar sense of bemusement. Despite the humorous tone she'd adopted, he suspected there was a very real trace of bitterness in her comment about men. He wondered who had hurt her and how high the wall was that she had built around her heart.

It didn't matter, he decided. He'd been climbing over everything from backyard fences to the hulking linemen of opposing teams his whole life. A few shaky feminine defenses shouldn't pose any kind of real hurdle at all.

Chapter Six

Beth wasn't sure what had made her insist on a 7:00 a.m. breakfast meeting with Ken. It was obvious the man didn't consider that a civilized hour for social chitchat or business talk. Maybe she was hoping to catch him while his brain was still a bit muddled. She liked the prospect of having the upper hand for once.

Or maybe she simply wanted to see him when his hair was still provocatively tousled from sleep, so she could let her imagination conjure up images of being beside him in bed. Gillie, who had taken one psychology class in college and considered herself an expert on human behavior, would have a field day with that one.

She had dressed with care. She had chosen a soft green sweater the shade of spring leaves to wear with her jeans. She'd slid her feet into a pair of flats and left her more practical boots and heavy socks in the car for the trip to the work site. She'd also caught herself taking extra care with her makeup. She had added a rare touch of eye shadow and mascara, even as she scolded herself for being ridiculous. She'd debated leaving her hair down, but at the last second she had wound it into a knot atop her head. As if to punish herself for her absurdity, she'd twisted it even tighter than usual.

Now, as she stood in the hallway outside Ken's suite, her stomach felt as fluttery as a teenager's on a first date. Only when she had spotted him beside his car the day before had she realized how much she had looked forward to his return. She was anticipating this breakfast even more and that terrified her. She knew where this breathless, edge-of-the-precipice feeling could lead—straight to heartache. Damn her lack of control over her own emotions and damn Gillie Townsend for encouraging her to risk everything on a man whose personal life was essentially a huge question mark.

She clutched her attaché case more tightly, reassured that there were enough papers inside to keep any conversation focused on business for the hour she had allotted for this meeting. Satisfied that for now she had her emotions and the next sixty minutes under control, she finally rapped on the door.

"Come on in. The door's open," he called from somewhere deep inside the suite.

Beth stepped through the doorway, then hesitated. Ken was nowhere in sight, which meant he was in the bedroom. Or perhaps he had just stepped out of the shower, his body still slick with water. Her blood sizzled as she considered that possibility. Heat climbed into her cheeks just as he poked his still-damp head around the door between the rooms.

"I'll be right out. Breakfast's on its way. Sign my name, if I'm not out when it gets here, okay?"

With her gaze fixed on the tiny sliver of bare chest she could glimpse through the partially closed door, she nodded. Unconscious of the gesture, she ran her tongue over her suddenly dry lips.

When she realized with a start that Ken's eyes had locked on her mouth, she blinked, then looked hurriedly away. She heard his deep chuckle as the door clicked shut. The man, blast him, obviously knew the effect he had on her. In fact, he probably deliberately set out to provoke her responses.

Fortunately, breakfast arrived just then, a rolling cart laden with fresh fruit, scrambled eggs, bacon, pancakes, toast, orange juice and coffee. She was still staring at it with open-mouthed amazement when Ken joined her.

She glanced at him. "Expecting an army?"

"I wasn't sure what you'd like. Besides, I always have a hearty appetite in the morning."

Unbidden, an image of his probably very busy nights filled with steamy sexual encounters flashed through her head. "I can imagine," she muttered.

He grinned, as if he had guessed the very wicked direction of her thoughts. He pulled out a chair for her at the table that had been set up in front of the window. As she sat, his fingers skimmed her shoulders, sending shock waves ricocheting through her. Such an innocent gesture to stir a response that was anything but innocent, she thought. To regain her equilibrium, she reached for her attaché case. Ken's hand closed over hers. Her heart thundered.

"Leave it," he commanded, his voice a whisper against her cheek. "Doing business over breakfast is bad for the digestion."

"I thought that was what power breakfasts were all about," Beth countered. "Besides, we don't have much time."

"Sure we do," he contradicted. "All day, in fact. I'm planning to come out to the house with you when we're through here."

"You can't," she said without thinking. How would she ever get anything done with him in plain sight, when she had barely been able to get him out of her head when he'd been in another state?

"Oh?" he said, regarding her with more amusement than offense.

She scrambled for an argument he wouldn't see straight through. "I mean, won't you be bored just standing around in the freezing cold watching other people work?"

"You do it all the time, don't you?"

"Yes, but it's my job."

"And it's my house. Besides, I intend to do more than stand around. I thought I'd pitch in."

She regarded him as if he had just announced an intention to build a skyscraper single-handedly. "Can you do that?"

"Depends on what needs doing, I suppose," he said cheerfully, his gaze challenging her to argue. He held out the platter of bacon and eggs. "Care for some?"

Beth shook her head. "No, the fruit and toast are just fine."

"That's not enough fuel for a cold day like this," he said, and plunked a spoonful of eggs and two strips of bacon on her plate. "Protein is essential."

She eyed the tempting but long-ago forbidden food warily. "Protein, maybe, but this is pure cholesterol."

"When was the last time you ate bacon and eggs?"

"I can't remember."

"Then you don't have to worry about the cholesterol just this once, do you?" he said, looking disgustingly pleased with his triumph. "Now, tell me how you ended up in Vermont."

With a faint sigh, Beth conceded to herself that she had completely lost control of this meeting, after all. Worse, she was beginning to relax under his patient, teasing questioning. And she knew what lay at the end of that road—trouble.

At the very least, she needed to put some distance between them. She had no intention of telling this man her life story. She kept her reply brief and unemotional.

"I had been skiing nearby one year," she said, avoiding any mention of how disastrous the trip had been with her stepchildren sulking the whole time and Peter blaming her for ruining the vacation.

"When I decided to leave California, I remembered how charmed I'd been by Berry Ridge when I'd driven through it one day."

She didn't add that she had taken the car for a ride while the rest of the family stayed at the ski resort. It was during that drive that she had reconciled herself to the fact that the marriage would never work. In fact, it had been over a cup of coffee and one of the Berry Ridge bakery's huge, warm cinnamon rolls that she had vowed to call it quits.

What had convinced her to move here was the fact that Lou Pulanski, the bakery's owner, had brought her the roll and refilled her coffee cup half a dozen times without any hint that she had noticed the tears streaking down Beth's cheeks. Oddly, Beth had found comfort in that quiet attention that had been offered without any attempt to intrude on her pain.

Now that she knew Lou better, she knew that the older woman would have been more than willing to lend an ear or to dispense advice, if asked. But she would never be so indiscreet as to suggest by word or deed that a customer might be in need of sympathy.

"Some folks just plain like to keep quiet about their troubles," she'd told Beth later. "If that's their choice, then I got no business not respecting it."

"What?" Ken said, interrupting her memories.

She regarded him blankly, unwillingly drawn back to the present.

"You were smiling. What were you thinking about?"

"How different Berry Ridge is from Los Angeles."

"You don't regret leaving the warm weather and sunshine for this?" He gestured out the window where more snow was falling against a leaden sky.

"It was a trade-off. No earthquakes, no traffic, and lots of serenity. What about you?"

"I've been on the east coast playing ball for more than ten years. I've gotten used to the cold. Chet Mathias had me up here one summer. I wasn't wild about the solitude at the time, but when I realized I was facing a long recovery from this injury, this seemed like the right place to do it. I figured maybe nobody around here would bother me." He shrugged. "I suppose it's too soon to tell if I'll like it enough to stay on."

Beth was surprised by the wistful note in his voice. She would have expected him to crave the recognition and adulation he'd had as a star quarterback, but she could definitely relate to his desire to keep to himself and recover. Perhaps they had more in common than she'd guessed. Both of them apparently viewed Berry Ridge as a haven, far from the turbulent life-styles they'd previously led.

"I guess Roger put an end to that notion right off the bat," she sympathized. "I'm sorry he was so tactless."

Ken shrugged. "He didn't mean any harm. Hopefully, though, he'll lay off those plans for some kind of football charity event."

"Fortunately, it will be months before the snow melts," she reassured him. "He'll probably forget all about it by then. Roger's enthusiasm is legendary in these parts, but he's fickle. He comes up with something new almost every day. If the town wants to follow through on one of his ideas, the mayor turns it over to a committee. Even the Chamber of Commerce, of which Roger's president, manages to snatch the reins away from him if it really wants to implement one of his ideas.''

She glanced at her watch. "Gracious, look at the time. I really do need to be going.''

"I'll drive you,'' he suggested.

"But my car...''

"Will be here when I bring you back.''

"What if you decide not to spend the whole day there?''

"I won't.''

To her amazement, Ken did stick it out. He even sent out for sandwiches and coffee for everyone at noon. And he graciously signed autographs for every single man before they left for the day. Initial awe and wariness had quickly given way to respect when he had, as promised, pitched in to help with whatever task was asked of him, no matter how menial.

"You've won them over,'' Beth said to him as they stood on the walkway after everyone else had gone. "You could complete this job without me.''

He glanced down at her and the expression in his eyes made her heart slam against her chest. "Not a chance,'' he said softly. "They'd figure out in no time that I don't have a clue about what needs to be done or how to do it.''

Beth seriously doubted the modest claim. He'd required almost no direction before he was handily repairing the molding in the master bedroom. In fact, at the rate the work was coming along, they really would have the repairs done and those two bedrooms ready with the basics by the following week. After that, most of the work would be cosmetic—wallpaper, paint, furniture, and those carefully chosen accessories and pictures that would make it seem like a home.

Still, it would take weeks to finish up. Weeks of working side by side with this man to whom she was drawn as inevitably as bits of metal to a magnet. Dangerous weeks.

She glanced up to find his gaze on her face. She lost herself in the warm expression in his eyes.

"Your hair is just about covered with snow," he said, his voice low.

Her entire body stilled as his fingers reached toward her hair. As light as his touch was, she could feel it all the way to her toes. And when the caress moved on to her cheek, she was convinced her heart would never withstand the thrill.

"Beth?"

"Hmm?" she murmured, her face upturned, her gaze locked with his as the pad of his thumb skimmed over her lower lip.

"Your skin is so hot, the snow melts as soon as it touches you."

She could believe that. In fact, she was burning up. She doubted her temperature would drop to normal until he took away his touch. She couldn't have dragged her gaze away from his for anything. Again her pulse skittered wildly as he slowly lowered his head. A halfhearted protest formed, but never made it past her lips as his mouth covered hers. Warmth spread through her, warmth and a kind of sweet torment.

She'd only had a heartbeat to anticipate the actual kiss, but somewhere deep inside she realized she had been anticipating it, dreaming about it, for days now. She had imagined the smooth texture of his lips, the fiery heat, the gentle persuasiveness. But none of her imaginings were nearly as devastating as the reality.

In reality, the kiss stole her breath, stole her good intentions, stole her powers of resistance. If her resolve and emotions were shaky, her body was alive with almost forgotten sensations. No, she corrected. She had never experienced anything quite like this before, after all. Every fiber of her being hummed...all from just one kiss.

Maybe if it had seemed practiced and assured, she wouldn't have fallen prey to it so easily. But his initial touch was uncertain, just hesitant enough to convince her that he hadn't expected this, either.

And in that instant of awareness, she felt the first faint stirring of trust. That was the most unexpected, most treasured sensation of all.

It had been seventy-two hours since the kiss.

Ken realized with chagrin that that was how he was beginning to mark time. Every minute, every hour that passed was traced back to the moment when he had lost his head and kissed Beth Callahan.

Damn, he felt as if he'd never kissed another woman before, when that was far from the truth. Not that he'd seduced anywhere near the numbers the tabloids printed. The fact of the matter was that he'd never seduced a soul other than his wife during his entire marriage. The vows had meant something to him, even in the last terrible months when he'd known in his gut the marriage was over.

Unfortunately, that commitment on his part hadn't prevented a lot of exuberant women from planting a kiss on him from time to time. Not one of those stolen kisses, not even the most enthusiastic and darkly sensual of them, had ever held a candle to the sweet surrender of Beth's lips beneath his.

Since the night when they'd stood in the snow, their bodies barely touching, but their mouths locked in a seductive dance, he hadn't laid so much as a finger on her. That resolve to back off hadn't stopped him from wanting to, though. In fact, he was losing patience with himself. He'd never allowed any woman to tie him in knots this way.

Like some randy kid, he had dreamed up excuse after excuse to spend the past three evenings with her. He had questioned prices, insisted on additional samples and, just the night before, had hauled her back to the house for a midnight inspection of some flaw that he claimed had been on his mind.

Standing on the front porch, bathed in moonlight, his body had ached with need for her, but he'd kept his hands firmly jammed into his pockets. He was proud of that restraint, that determined refusal to take what he wanted, not even another kiss. He wasn't nearly as proud of having dragged her out at that hour in the first place.

She had responded to his irrational demands with patience and good humor. In fact, she was so blasted calm and serene, he found it irritating. Hadn't she felt what he'd felt? Hadn't she been as stunned as he was by the force of a desire barely held in check?

Apparently not, he decided as she quietly handed him yet another set of unnecessary figures.

Avoiding her gaze, he decided enough was enough. Once the house was finished, he would avoid the lingering dinners that somehow always seemed to follow their business meetings. In fact, he would avoid anything more than a casual greeting on the street. That would be best . . . for both of them. He needed to concentrate on his daughter now. Beth needed peace of mind.

In the meantime, every time they saw each other he felt a terrible longing to kiss her again, to loosen her hair and watch it tumble free, to unbutton the top button of her high-necked blouse . . . and then the next . . . and the next.

Damn, but he'd better finish the initial redecorating and get an increasingly impatient and belligerent Chelsea up here before he made an utter fool of himself and did something he'd regret. Berry Ridge was too small. He would have to face up to a mistake with Beth Callahan every single day of his life. And she, no doubt, would pay an even higher price for his lack of sensible restraint, especially if things didn't work out in Berry Ridge and he moved away to someplace better for Chelsea.

He glanced down into her green eyes, as luminous as emeralds, and felt his resolve waver. Again.

"I've been thinking," he said, his voice husky with unspoken need.

She regarded him expectantly. "About what?"

"I read that there's a big antique auction this weekend. I thought maybe we should go. What do you think?"

She beamed at him and his heart flipped over. "I have the notice in my purse. I was thinking the same thing."

"Great minds..." he murmured.

"We can stop by some shops, too, and you can see the pieces I had in mind firsthand before you make a decision."

"Sounds perfect," he said. A whole day, alone, together. It did sound perfect.

It also sounded more dangerous than facing down an all-pro line dead set on stripping him of a football and planting his rear on a rock-hard field. To his everlasting regret, he could hardly wait.

Chapter Seven

Saturday dawned with cloudless blue skies, relatively mild temperatures in the thirties and endless stretches of snowy landscape. It was the kind of postcard-perfect morning that reminded Beth why all the subzero temperatures were worth tolerating.

For once she didn't think about Ken as she chose her clothes: a pair of sturdy denims, a turtleneck topped by a flannel shirt, boots, and a down-lined jacket. Though the auction itself was indoors, many of the places they planned to visit would have items on display outdoors or in unheated barns. She didn't intend to miss anything, no matter how chilly the air or how many filthy things had to be moved out of the way. An antique lover had to be part dreamer, part expert and part intrepid adventurer. She wasn't entirely sure which mattered most. She, for one, liked the adventure of it best.

Until she'd come to Vermont she had never known the joy of discovering a genuine treasure buried amid piles of dilapidated furniture or time-worn utensils. The process of discovery was almost as rewarding as taking some beloved object home. She enjoyed talking to the knowledgeable dealers, learning more with each contact until she was now able to spot quality amid junk. She loved sorting through a clutter of items and imagining the people who'd once lovingly held even the most garish knickknack in their hands. She got a real adrenaline rush from the competitive bidding. Her excitement mounted just thinking about the day ahead.

And that was even before she added Ken into the mix.

She brewed a pot of coffee and poured it into a thermos, then put that into the basket she'd already filled with Lou's bakery-fresh blueberry muffins, napkins and two mugs. That should tide them over through lunch. And the coffee would take the chill off while they were exploring all of the prospective finds at the auction.

She hoped that Ken proved to be a patient companion. She'd been known to linger through hours of bidding just to get her hands on some two-dollar treasure she'd spotted lumped in with an entire lot of pure junk.

By the time her doorbell finally rang, she was already pacing, anxious to hit the road to see what the day had to offer. Basket in hand, checkbook in her purse, she opened the door and all thoughts of antiques died, driven straight out of her head by one quick glance at the sexy man on her doorstep. Lordy, but he took her breath away—a fact that deeply troubled her.

"Good morning," he said, seemingly oblivious to the impact he had on her.

"Morning," she mumbled when she managed to find her tongue. This wasn't good. If the man could render her speechless just by showing up, exactly what would happen if he ever actively set out to seduce her? She sure as heck hoped he would try soon so she could end the speculation and then get on with her life. Trying to figure out why that one knockout of a kiss hadn't been repeated was tormenting her.

He reached for the basket and drew in a deep breath. "Coffee?" She nodded. "Thank you. You've saved my life. Maybe we should have a cup here before we hit the road," he said, regarding her hopefully.

"No," Beth said curtly, then winced. "Sorry. It's just that we don't want to be late. I want to get a look at everything before the bidding starts."

"You take this stuff seriously, don't you?"

"You should, too," she advised him. "It's your money we're spending." She closed the door and headed to the driveway. "Let's go. You can drink your coffee on the road."

She realized he wasn't following and turned back. "What's wrong?"

"I was just wondering if you ever slow down and have fun."

She grinned at his worried tone. "This *is* fun," she promised. "You'll see. I guarantee that before the day is out you're going to buy something ridiculous that you don't need, just for the sheer thrill of acquiring it."

"Bet I don't," he countered. "Talk to my broker. He'll tell you I'm thoughtful and disgustingly methodical when I look into a new stock acquisition. I have never, *ever* taken an impetuous, uncalculated risk."

"Want to lay odds that you will today?" Beth challenged.

"Sure," he said with supreme confidence. "If I win, you'll spend an entire evening with me. Dinner, dancing, the works. Not one mention of the house or its contents will cross your lips."

She was taken aback by his choice, but she was too much of a competitor to back away. "And if I win?"

"You won't," he said confidently.

"But if I do?"

"You choose."

She thought about what she wanted most at this precise moment on a Saturday morning in early November. "If I win, I want you to come to my place, fix a huge bowl of buttered popcorn, pour some nice white wine—"

"I'm beginning to like the sound of this," he taunted. "Maybe I should let you win."

"Stop," she said, laughing. "I'm not finished." Her expression sobered and she studied him worriedly. "You may not like this."

"Try me," he said, apparently not fazed by her suddenly troubled tone.

"I want you to play a videotape of one of your Super Bowl victories."

He regarded her incredulously. "Why would you want me to do that?" he asked, his voice suddenly dull and lifeless, all the joy drained out of it.

"I want to see for myself how great you were."

"Past tense," he reminded her. "You know who I am now. Why does any of that matter?"

Beth wasn't sure she could explain, short of admitting that over the past few days she had felt an increasing need to know everything about him. Football seemed a safer topic than his personal life.

"Because football was a huge part of your life. It shaped you. I'd like to understand that." Unwilling to explain further, or to admit to feelings that she wasn't ready to put a name to, she met his gaze evenly. "If it's still too painful, I can wait a while longer."

"But you won't just forget about it."

She shook her head. "Afraid not."

Suddenly his expression brightened and he winked. "Or I can just win the bet."

Relieved that her request hadn't spoiled the mood, Beth grinned at him. "Not a chance, Hutchinson. Not a chance. You're too much of a competitor to let anything you want get away."

His gaze caught hers and held, the challenge plain and far more seductive than she'd anticipated. "I hope you will always remember that, Beth."

Her heart climbed into her throat as their gazes remained locked. The bet faded in importance. All that mattered now was the intent of that quiet warning. Ken had just reminded her with a few spare words that there was more at stake in the game they were playing than a few stolen kisses. She trembled at the realization that whatever the stakes, he was a man whose entire public persona revolved around winning.

Ken gazed around the jam-packed auction house with a sense of amazement. It looked to him as if every farmer, every Yuppie, and every slick antique dealer from a two-hundred-mile radius or even farther had turned out.

He stood in line with Beth to purchase a number, chuckling when she insisted he have his own.

"If I'm paying for everything, why can't we share?" he grumbled without any real rancor, loving this lighthearted mood she was in.

"Because when you go nuts and start bidding, I want that number of yours on record so there won't be any reneging on our bet." Suddenly all business, she pulled a notebook from her purse. "Now, are you coming with me or do you plan to look around on your own?"

"Hey, this is all new to me. I'd better stick with my instructor."

She grinned at him. "Just try not to fall behind. We only have an hour to see everything."

"I'll do my best," he promised, trying to keep the amusement out of his voice. After all, there was absolutely nothing in this huge room that could possibly compete with the woman he was with. She was just about the most fascinating person on the face of the planet, as near as he could tell. He loved her whole-hearted enthusiasm for whatever task she was engaged in. More and more, he was wishing that driven intensity would be focused on him. Not his house. Not the furnishings. Not these antiques. Not any of the other myriad things that distracted her. Just him.

His gaze rarely left her as they surveyed a pile of rusty beds. It never strayed as they tried the doors and drawers on a dozen different dressers and cabinets. Most of them had warped wood and layers of paint, as near as he could tell.

Beth definitely held his attention as they edged between stacks of old quilts that, despite their intricate beauty, smelled musty to him. And she was far more intriguing than a bunch of old pictures, most of which couldn't even be seen through the coating of dust on frames and glass.

Then he saw the old-fashioned sleigh. Its runners were rusty. The paint was chipped and peeling. The leather upholstery was weathered beyond repair.

But when he looked at it, he remembered every Christmas card he'd ever seen with a Currier and Ives winter scene. He envisioned that sleigh with its runners gleaming, its upholstery buttersoft and comfortable, its paint a shiny black trimmed with gold and a pair of prancing horses pulling it through the snow.

Chelsea would be entranced, he thought at once. But it wasn't his daughter he imagined bundled up in blankets as the sleigh moved across the pure white Vermont landscape. It was Beth, snuggled by his side on a romantic, starlit night.

"Well, I'll be damned!" he muttered to himself as he ran his fingers over the sleigh and marveled at his sudden flight of fancy.

Two hours later the decrepit sleigh was brought up to the front of the auction house.

Ken listened to the first bid to get an idea of the value. Fifty dollars. He would pay ten times that or more, he decided. He stayed out of it until the price hit two hundred and fifty.

"Five hundred," he called out, holding his number aloft as he'd seen others do.

Beth's head snapped around and she regarded him with wide-eyed astonishment. "What are you doing?" she asked, trying to tug his arm down.

"I want it."

"It's falling apart," she told him in a hushed voice.

"I want it," he repeated stubbornly.

Suddenly a slow, delighted smile spread across her face and whatever argument she'd planned to offer died on her lips. She released her grip on his arm. "Go for it, then."

He bought the sleigh for six hundred and fifty dollars and considered it a bargain. He didn't even want to know what it was really worth. Only when the bidding was over and he'd written his check and gone outside to claim the sleigh did he stare at it with a sense of bemusement. He turned to Beth.

"Now what do I do with it to make it go?"

Her quick peal of laughter rang out on the crisp air and in seconds he had joined in. "Promise you'll go for the first ride with me when it's fixed," he coaxed.

She glanced from the sleigh to him and back again. "You'll be lucky to get this thing cleaned up and usable by next winter."

Ken shook his head. "You're forgetting that I have a miracle worker on my payroll. Consider this your first priority."

Her eyebrows quirked up. "Before the house?"

"Before everything," he said softly. "Except this."

His lips met hers in a quick claiming, then lingered to savor her startled sigh, the velvet-soft texture of her mouth and the warm moistness inside. His entire body trembled with a fierce longing for even more, but he slowly pulled away, shaken by the force of his growing feelings for this woman who had been a stranger only a few weeks before.

His gaze settled on the flashing sparks in her green eyes. "I wish..."

"What?" she said, sounding faintly breathless from an anticipation that he sensed matched his own.

"That we were somewhere other than the middle of a snowy parking lot, someplace cozy and warm and intimate."

Her eyes widened, then darkened with what he was now certain was a desire as powerful as his. He could feel the quickening of the pulse in her neck beneath his fingertips, the slow, unmistakable heating of her skin. "Beth?"

"Hmm?"

"Is that a possibility?"

For an instant he sensed that she was at war with herself. Then a sigh seemed to shudder through her and she slowly nodded. "My place," she said in a voice barely above a whisper.

The answer might have been succinct, a little hesitant, but he knew a commitment when he heard one. He sensed there would be no second thoughts. He pressed another kiss against her lips, headed off to make arrangements for the delivery of the sleigh, then practically ran back to the car, praying all the while that he was right and that she wouldn't change her mind.

He wouldn't blame her if she did. Even if she'd never heard of him before, surely over the past few weeks she'd heard about his reputation for supposedly torrid, love-'em-and-leave-'em affairs. The whole town was abuzz with such gossip and a lot more speculation about him. The tabloid lies were something he'd come to take for granted, but he didn't want Beth believing them, not for one single minute. He wanted her to understand that whatever happened between them would be as rare and special for him as he guessed it would be for her. He wanted her to know, even if he didn't understand how or why it had happened, that she mattered to him, that because of her he was healing, learning who he was again.

If only he could find the words.

All the way back to Berry Ridge, Beth prayed that Ken wouldn't say another word. She didn't want him to manufacture pretty speeches or to make promises that he wouldn't keep. It was enough that right now, at this moment, they both wanted the same thing. They both wanted to explore this wild, reckless longing that had sprung up, unanticipated and unwanted, but undeniable in its fierce intensity.

Ken Hutchinson had somehow sneaked into a heart she'd been so certain had turned to ice. It was enough that there was fire and passion back in her life again, that she felt desirable and alive. She needed this proof that no matter how badly she had failed as a stepmother, she had not failed as a woman. She would deal with the consequences soon enough and she didn't want that process complicated by a longing to believe words spoken in haste. She had convinced herself of one thing—Ken was an honorable man. If he hadn't mentioned a wife by now, one didn't exist. She supposed she should have asked directly, but this was one time she was going to go with her gut instinct.

Ken drove with a sort of savage intensity, his brow knit in concentration as he guided the four-wheel drive wagon over narrow roads with a thin, dangerous coating of ice. The trip seemed to last forever, fraying Beth's nerves more with each mile. She concentrated on the road, because she feared if she thought about the step they were about to take her resolve would falter. She didn't want to be robbed of a chance to experience just once the pleasure of making love to a man whose loyalties and attention weren't divided by other obligations as Peter's had been from the outset of their relationship.

She caught Ken's quick, sideways glance, then felt his gloved hand wrap around her own and squeeze reassuringly. "I could slow down or change direction," he offered, and won her heart completely.

"I'd have to shoot you if you did," she retorted lightly, drawing a smile.

Within seconds his expression sobered. "I'm serious, Beth. This doesn't have to happen today or even tomorrow. It will happen, though."

Grateful for the option to say no, she declined it nonetheless. "Today," she repeated with more assurance, reading into the promise of someday a statement about his availability being uncompromised.

He nodded and turned his full attention back to the slippery road for the remainder of the drive.

It was late afternoon by the time they pulled into Beth's driveway. Low, dark clouds promising a new snowfall and an early dusk hung over the horizon, shutting out the last pale rays of sun.

Inside the house, Ken immediately set about lighting a fire, while Beth tried to settle her jitters in the kitchen. She opened a bottle of crisp Chardonnay and poured it into her best crystal wineglasses. She put a bunch of grapes on a tray, along with a round of Brie and an assortment of crackers. To that she added a fat green candle, scented with evergreen, telling herself it would seem as if they were making love in a forest clearing or in the final, magical hours of Christmas Eve. Then she chided herself for the whimsical, romantic thought.

The only thing she couldn't bring herself to do was to slip upstairs and shed her dusty clothes and trade them for delicate, lacy lingerie. Somehow it seemed as if that would be too calculated, hastening a process that deserved slow, deliberate and ever-more-thrilling seduction.

After setting the tray on the coffee table, she found herself suddenly at a loss. Ken was stretched out on the carpet in front of the fire. The sofa was too far away for any sort of intimacy. It seemed as if even conversation would grow stilted across that chasm. And surely no quiet secrets or whispered words could be shared.

Ending her dilemma, Ken held up a hand and tugged her down beside him.

"I like your house. The warm colors suit you," he told her, brushing a stray tendril of hair back from her face. "It feels like a home."

Beth's breath snagged in her throat, but she managed a shaky "Thanks." Even that much was a struggle with every touch assaulting her senses. She felt one pin come out of her hair, then another and another, until the careful knot she'd twisted on top of her head that morning was undone. Ken's gaze was rapt as he ran his fingers through the curly strands until they had tumbled free to her shoulders.

"It looks exactly the way I'd imagined," he whispered. "Why do you always wear it up?"

Beth shrugged as if the styling of her hair were of no consequence, even though she knew that she had chosen it deliberately because it seemed less feminine, less likely to entice masculine attention. "It keeps it out of my face when I'm working."

He looked doubtful. "Are you sure that's it?"

"What else could it be?" she asked, even though she knew herself that it wasn't the whole truth, but merely as much as she was willing to admit.

"I thought maybe it was like all that bulky tweed and those prim blouses you wore when we first met."

Startled by his perceptiveness, she met his eyes, then looked away in embarrassment.

"So, that was it," he said softly. "Why were you trying to hide? Didn't you realize that no matter what you wore, no one could mistake you for anything other than a very attractive, very sexy woman? Why would you even want to disguise that? Who made you afraid of your own sensuality?"

Beth didn't want to think about the past or the failures that had driven her to retreat from relationships. She only wanted to think about here and now. About this man and being held in his arms. Who better to reassure her than a man who wasn't looking for commitment, a man whose amorous adventures had been bandied around town ever since his arrival? She wanted passion, not love. Or so she told herself.

Without saying a word, she reached out and cupped a hand behind his neck and drew his head forward until their mouths met. As she'd hoped, that gesture was all it took to end conversation, to drive out thoughts of anything else.

The slow, experimental kisses soon exploded into desperate, frantic need. Ken, who up until now had seemed endlessly patient, suddenly indulged only in caresses meant to inflame. The swift, sure strokes of his hands drove out everything except the way her body was melting under his touch.

Clothes miraculously disappeared, leaving firelight to dance across bare flesh glistening with a sheen of perspiration. There was no time to linger over the masculine perfection of his body, because her own was filled with this increasingly urgent demand.

"Do you like this?" he murmured, his fingers slick with her own moisture.

A nod, because there was no breath to speak.

"And this?"

"Oh, yes," she whispered, the words choked.

"Tell me, Beth. Tell me what you need."

She moaned softly and because the words still wouldn't come, she showed him, guiding his hands and then his body until he was deep inside her and the world was spinning, topsy-turvy around them.

It seemed like forever before the spinning slowed and the world righted itself. But even though her senses calmed to something more like normal, Beth knew that nothing would ever be quite the same again.

As impossible as it seemed, as untimely as it was, she had just discovered magic.

Chapter Eight

Ken wondered if there was anything more complicated in the entire realm of human relationships than waking up next to a person for the very first time after a night of making love. He studied the woman curled up next to him in the cramped bed meant for two people who never budged all night. They had done considerably more than that, he thought, smiling at the memories. And Beth continued to look radiant and desirable, even asleep.

What a delightfully sexy, unexpected treasure Beth Callahan had turned out to be! He had no idea where things with the two of them were headed. In fact, if anyone had suggested just a few short days ago that he would contemplate an affair, much less anything more serious, for years to come, he would have argued vehemently against the possibility. Hell, he'd told himself that in no uncertain terms. But with every day that had passed, he'd become increasingly certain that Beth was too special not to see what the future for them held.

Only days ago his life had seemed too chaotic and unsettled, his daughter in need of too much attention, to bring anyone else into their lives. He had anticipated a long road toward physical and emotional healing for both of them. Instead he suddenly seemed to be looking ahead, not back. The career-ending injury to his knee seemed less and less important except as an inconvenience or irritant. The breakup of his marriage saddened him, but apparently hadn't incapacitated his desire to reach out to another woman, after all.

Quite probably, the very fact that Beth clearly hadn't expected or wanted this to happen, either, had made it possible. After years of being married to a woman who'd manipulated everything, no matter how trivial, finding a woman as straightforward and honest as Beth had broken through his defenses. There wasn't one single shred of doubt in his mind that she wanted nothing from him—not his money, not the reflected light of his celebrity, most likely not even his permanence in her life. To his astonishment, he realized he trusted her more after these past few days than he had ever trusted Pam.

Not that that was saying much, he conceded ruefully. It hadn't taken him long to realize that his ex-wife would use any tactic it took, other than a straight-out request, to get what she wanted. Apparently it was some sort of game for her. A psychologist would probably point out that a woman with Pam's insecurities couldn't believe that asking alone would bring the desired results.

What no one had ever explained to Ken's satisfaction was why a woman as beautiful and intelligent as his ex-wife, a woman who had come from a loving home, would lack self-assurance in the first place. Perhaps he should have tried harder early in the marriage to find out, but he hadn't and it was too late now. Maybe Pam would find in Hollywood what she hadn't found with him—her self-esteem.

Though he knew very little at this moment about what his future held, he did know that the one thing he would not tolerate in a woman again were lies and subterfuge. Beth Callahan seemed incapable of either. Just being with her put him at ease, knowing there was no need to look for hidden agendas behind every word and act.

One thing did puzzle him, though. She had never once expressed any interest in his personal life. Maybe she knew all she needed to know from the tabloids and the gossips in town, but he doubted that was it. If that was where she was getting her information, he doubted they would be in this bed together now.

He wondered how she was going to feel when she discovered he had custody of a seven-year-old daughter. He hoped it would delight her. They hadn't discussed her culinary skills, but he had a hunch Beth could bake those cookies Chelsea pouted about not having whenever Delores Jensen wasn't around to make them for her.

Well, he would know soon enough how his daughter's presence would alter their relationship. Delores was going to bring Chelsea up to Vermont next weekend. Chelsea's rebelliousness was showing signs of fading just as soon as the finishing touches were put on the first rooms in the new house. Beth had promised they would be ready by midweek, which would give him time to move his own things over from the inn. Perhaps they'd even have a night or two there alone. He knew that no matter how things changed, he would never be able to walk through the rooms of his new home without envisioning Beth there, as well.

Of course, why waste time anticipating the future when the present was so intriguing? He slid a hand under the covers and skimmed it lightly over Beth's warm curves. The touch brought a faint smile to her lips. He pressed a kiss against her bare shoulder and earned a soft moan. A caress of her breast brought her eyes open and quickly had them smoldering with reawakened passion.

Or so he thought, until she yawned and stretched, the movement as lazy and satisfied as a cat's.

"So, you find my attention boring, do you?" he taunted, intensifying his touch until she gasped.

"Never," she whispered, her voice breathless.

"What was that?" he asked again.

Her body arched toward him as he continued to explore. "Definitely...not...boring."

He grinned. "That's better."

She reached for him then and the provocative game immediately reversed, until they were both slick with perspiration, their breath coming in gasps, their bodies demanding a fulfillment that finally came with shattering intensity.

When their heartbeats had slowed and their skin had cooled, Beth stretched out alongside him, their bodies touching from shoulder to toe. Somehow that innocent, trusting contact of two satiated bodies seemed more intimate, more profound than the love-making itself. Ken discovered he was relishing the aftermath of sex as much as the act itself. It was a sensation he'd long forgotten. It had been lost sometime after he'd discovered how deliberately and coolly Pam had used her body to get what she wanted. And though he'd seldom been able to resist, he'd hated himself for the loveless unions.

Whatever happened between him and Beth over the coming weeks and months, he would be grateful to her for this moment, for reminding him of the simple joy of genuine togetherness between a man and a woman who wanted nothing more complicated from each other than to give and receive this incredible, most basic of all pleasures.

"You know, it's a strange thing, my man," Claude Dobbins said to Ken first thing Monday morning. "I called you at this quiet, isolated country inn two or three times Saturday night. Clear up till midnight, in fact. I coulda sworn you told me they rolled up the sidewalks there at nine o'clock."

Ken guessed where this conversation was heading. He attempted a diversion. "Maybe I should be telling the coach about his key offensive lineman staying up past curfew the night before a game."

"Don't you go trying to change the subject," Dobbins said, not taking the bait. "I called you again right before I left for the stadium Sunday morning. No answer in your suite. No sign of you downstairs in the restaurant. In fact, do you know what the incredibly helpful dude at the front desk told me?"

Ken could see they were going to play this conversation all the way to the end, no matter what he did. He decided he might as well relax and let Dobbins have his fun.

"I can't imagine," he said, praying that his friend hadn't shared this speculation with Delores. His goose would be cooked then.

"That man said you'd left on Saturday morning and he hadn't seen you since. He said you had a nice little stack of messages that hadn't been picked up, either."

"Good work, Sherlock," Ken said dryly.

Dobbins ignored the sarcasm. "Now, I know for a fact you didn't come down to see your kid, because I stopped by to see Delores and give her a cake Harriet had baked. She said she wasn't expecting you at all this week. She said she'd be moving Chelsea up to Vermont next weekend and you were busy getting things ready."

"All true. What's your point?"

"Well, I got to thinking. What would keep a man who doesn't know beans about decorating hanging around an empty house? And you know what I decided?"

"I can't imagine."

"I decided it seemed real likely that, despite all of your denials, you do have a thing for that real estate person."

"I thought I explained to you this real estate person is just working for me."

"After hours?"

"What makes you so sure I was with Beth? Maybe I was out with Chet Mathias."

"No way, man. He's out of the country. I called his house, too, and talked to the housekeeper."

"You are one nosy son of a . . ."

Claude laughed. "Come on, now. Tell the truth."

"About what?"

"Were you engaging in a little hanky-panky with the hired help?"

"Dobbins, my man, I don't believe that's any of your business."

"Me and Harriet weren't none of your business, either. Didn't stop you from messin' with *my* life."

"You have a very short memory. That was Delores at work, not me. I just stood on the sidelines and watched."

"You still haven't answered my question."

"That's right," Ken agreed cheerfully. "Did you have some reason for calling? Other than jerking my chain, that is?"

Dobbins's laughter boomed over the line. "My man, I am not finished with this subject. Not by a long shot. However, I will delay that particular discussion for another time. I called because I thought you ought to know that Chelsea is giving Delores fits. Threw an outright tantrum while I was there on Saturday for a few minutes. Over nothing, as near as I could tell. Didn't want no part of me. Wouldn't touch the cake. Finally stormed off to her room.''

Ken's spirits sank. Chelsea adored Claude. For her to display a fit of temper when he'd come to visit was totally out of character. What was happening to his lovely, good-natured daughter? ''Delores hasn't said anything to me and I've called there to talk to Chelsea every day.''

''She wouldn't. She knows you've got a lot on your mind now. And she thinks this thing with Chelsea will pass once the two of you are settled in Vermont. I'm thinking maybe you ought to bite the bullet and give Pam a call and see if you can't get her to call her daughter.''

The very idea of speaking to his ex-wife made Ken's stomach churn. Unfortunately, however, he couldn't argue with his friend's logic, especially since he had a hunch it was advice straight from Harriet, who was a school counselor and very wise in the ways of troublesome kids.

''I assume Harriet agrees with you.''

''More like me agreeing with her,'' Dobbins admitted. ''If ever there was a kid missing her mama, that child of yours is it. If you don't want to call Pam, Delores would probably do it, though the way she's feeling about her daughter these days, it doesn't seem to me like that's such a good idea.''

''It's not. Besides, it's my responsibility. Thanks, buddy. I owe you for letting me know about this. I'll call Chelsea after school today myself and I'll see that Pam does, too.''

"You coming home soon? We got a place of honor for you on the sidelines anytime."

"I don't think I'm much suited for watching the action from the sidelines. Besides, this is home now."

Even after he had hung up, Ken couldn't get the words he'd spoken out of his head. This *was* home now. And in large measure, that was due to Beth's presence. He could only pray that Chelsea would quickly come to feel the same way.

He glanced at his watch. It was barely 7:00 a.m. in California, no doubt a good time to catch Pam. She'd probably be sound asleep and irritable at being awakened. However, it also meant she'd be too muddled to give him much aggravation.

The phone rang half a dozen times before being tumbled off the hook and sent clattering to the floor. He held the receiver away from his ear, prepared for the impending burst of anger.

"What the hell?" she muttered grumpily when she finally had phone in hand. "Who is this?"

"Ken."

Silence greeted him, then a calmer, but no more friendly, "What do you want?"

"When was the last time you talked to Chelsea?"

"Last week. The week before. I can't remember exactly. It's the middle of the night, for God's sake. Ask me again at noon."

"Dammit, Pam. You're her mother. Even if you don't give a damn about her, she misses you. Would it be too much trouble for you to take five minutes to speak to her every couple of days while she's adjusting to all the changes we're dragging her through?"

"What about you? Last time I called, I heard you hadn't been home for days."

He drew in a deep breath and prayed for patience. "Look, I'm sorry. Let's not let this disintegrate into an exchange of accusations, okay? She'll be up here with me by this weekend. I talk to her once or twice a day. It's not me she's missing. It's you."

"Okay, okay. I get the message."

"You'll call her this afternoon?"

"I'm going out on an audition. I'm not sure when I'll have time."

"Make time, dammit," he retorted, then slammed down the phone before he got into a futile shouting match with her despite his best intentions.

When his pulse rate had returned to normal, he sent a brief gaze heavenward and gave thanks that he was only a few days away from having Chelsea with him, only a few days away from getting a little stability back into both their lives.

On Wednesday afternoon, barely two weeks after they'd started work on the remodeling of the Grady place, thanks to whirlwind activity and persuasive charm, the master bedroom was at least livable, even if the rest of the house was still in disarray.

Though Beth had seen Ken nightly all week long, he hadn't stopped by to check on progress. He'd said the workmen were better off left alone to get the job done, rather than training him in the process. She had a feeling, though, that he had suddenly wanted to put at least a little distance between them so they could both examine what was happening with some semblance of rationality.

Personally, though, she didn't want to think. For the first time in a very long time, she was content simply to feel. She could hardly wait for him to see the finished room, could hardly wait, in fact, to join him in the extravagant king-size bed he'd insisted he had to have.

"It's ready," she had told him on Wednesday night as they lay entwined amid the rumpled sheets and quilts on her own bed. "Can you come by in the morning?"

"Make it afternoon and I'll be there," he had suggested. "In fact, why don't you give the crew the afternoon off and we'll celebrate."

Her pulse had skittered wildly at the provocative glint in his eyes, even though it had been only moments since they had made love with so much passion and abandon that her body still ached from it.

With his eyes hooded and his gaze locked with hers, he'd said huskily, "In the meantime . . ."

As she thought back, a smile tugged at her lips. In the meantime, there had definitely been plenty to occupy their time.

Now, though, as she waited for Ken to arrive, she paced nervously through the debris still littering the downstairs. What if he hated the navy blue carpet? Or the pin-striped cream and navy wallpaper? Or the antique oak furniture? Oh, sure, he'd chosen it with her, but there was a vast difference between a small sample of something and a finished room. She could envision the end results with no difficulty, but what if he hadn't been able to and was disappointed?

Filled with doubts and anticipation, she took the chilled bottle of champagne from the refrigerator, picked up the two glasses she'd brought from home and carried them upstairs. She was still there, fiddling unnecessarily with the hang of the drapes, when she heard his car pull into the driveway. With her breath caught in her throat, she waited where she was.

"Beth?"

His shout echoed through the mostly empty house.

"Up here."

She heard his footsteps on the uncarpeted stairs. Hampered by his injured knee, his progress wasn't nearly as fast as she would have liked. Hands clasped tightly, she met him in the doorway.

His arms came around her at once, gathering her close. His clothes and his skin were cold against her, but she could feel the warmth radiating from deep inside and knew that within seconds they would both be on fire and the purpose of this visit would fade. Reluctantly, she stepped away.

"Oh, no, you don't," she said. "You at least have to look around first."

"Trust me. I'll see the bed soon enough," he said, reaching for her again.

Beth couldn't recall anyone ever being so hungry for her. His desire was exhilarating. And tempting. The battle to resist was a real struggle, but one she ultimately won.

"Ken Hutchinson, I did not lure you over here just so you could test the bed."

A grin spread across his face. "Okay, I get it. First, I praise your work. *Then* I get to sample it."

"Something like that."

"Then let's get this tour over with."

Beth pulled him into the room, then stood aside. With far more invested in his reaction than simple professional pride, she watched avidly as his expression changed from unexpectant to astonished and finally to delight.

"You're a miracle worker," he enthused, hauling her into his arms and planting a kiss on her forehead.

Beth's pulse bucked with what had become a predictable stirring of excitement, then seemed to skid to a halt. Her gaze flew to his. He looked just as stunned as she felt. His eyes focused on her mouth, then lifted to meet her gaze. Then slowly, ever so slowly, his lips covered hers in a kiss that quickly left her pliant and fuzzy-headed.

That incredible moment lasted for an eternity, then he was reaching for the hem of her sweater and tugging it up, sprinkling kisses across the bare flesh of her midriff. Beth was lost in the sweet, wild abandon of his touch when she heard the creak of the door downstairs. Her entire body froze.

"Did you hear that?"

"What?" he murmured distractedly.

She pushed him away and straightened her sweater. "Somebody just came in downstairs."

"I didn't hear anything."

"I did," she insisted. "Maybe one of the crew came back for something."

He sighed. "You won't be satisfied until we check this out, will you?"

"Afraid not."

He cast a longing look at the champagne, then at the bed and finally at her. "Damn, but I was looking forward to trying out that bed."

She grinned at the plaintive note in his voice. "Me, too, but it will still be here when we come back upstairs."

"You could just climb into bed and wait for me," he suggested hopefully. "I'd like to think about finding you there, naked, anxious."

"Oh, no," she said, forcing herself to ignore temptation in favor of common sense. "I don't want to explain what I'm doing there, if whoever it is gets past you."

"It won't happen, but come along if it'll make you happy."

They started down the stairs together. As they neared the bottom, at a cautionary gesture from Ken, Beth hung back. The position gave her an excellent view of the foyer and the living room beyond. In fact, she was perfectly positioned when a towheaded child wearing a velvet-collared coat, black patent leather shoes and fur earmuffs came barreling through the archway from the living room and threw herself straight into Ken's arms.

Beth watched the smile break across his face, saw him gather the child close and pepper her face with kisses until she was giggling with delight. Beth's heart thudded dully in her chest as she took in the scene with a deepening sense of dread and betrayal.

Maybe she was wrong. Maybe this wasn't Ken's child, a child he had never once mentioned. Maybe, she thought, as the sinking sensation spread through her.

But the gray eyes, the strong chin, the exuberant greeting said otherwise. So did the glow of parental pride and pleasure in Ken's expression.

If those things alone hadn't convinced Beth of the relationship, the child's first comment ended speculation.

"Daddy!" she said, an expression of dismay on her little face as she surveyed the downstairs of the house. "Do we really have to live here? This place is a mess."

Daddy, Beth repeated to herself, more hurt by that single word than the childish disdain for the house she loved. What terrible twist of fate had allowed her to begin falling in love with yet another man who already had a child?

Chapter Nine

Holding his daughter in his arms, Ken took one look at Beth's pale, stricken face and wondered what on earth was wrong. He realized that Chelsea and Delores, who must be in the living room, couldn't have turned up at a worse time, but Beth looked stunned. In fact, when she finally shifted her gaze to meet his, he could have sworn what he saw in her eyes was a terrible accusation of betrayal.

Before he could react, before he could offer an explanation or even introduce her to Chelsea, she whirled and ran into the kitchen.

"Who was that lady?" Chelsea demanded.

"That was Beth Callahan. She's the lady who helped me find the house," he said just as Delores came in from the living room, her eyes twinkling, apparently at the mention of Beth.

"So where is she? I'm dying to get a look at her," she teased. "Of course, judging from that color in your cheeks, maybe I should be asking what the two of you were doing upstairs when we arrived and why you didn't have sense enough to lock the front door."

He scowled at his ex-mother-in-law, hoping the look was fierce enough to put an end to that bit of speculation, particularly with his precocious daughter listening in. Unfortunately, there wasn't the slightest sign of repentance in her expression. If anything, she looked even more fascinated by his reaction to the question.

"She went into the kitchen for something," Ken said, glancing worriedly in that direction. He wondered if she would scoot straight out the back door or come back so that she could meet his family.

"I hope you don't mind that we came a day early," Delores said, finally dropping her teasing. "Chelsea was getting anxious. Her teacher told me she wasn't paying a bit of attention in school, anyway."

"We wanted to surprise you, Daddy."

He hugged her. "I'm glad you did, Shortstuff." He just wished they had turned up an hour or two from now. More, he wished that Beth had been more prepared for the arrival.

It was his own damn fault. He should have discussed his situation with her, even if she'd never asked about it. Probably no woman, however much she might like kids, wanted to have one sprung on her the way Chelsea had turned up here today.

It was also entirely possible that Beth was simply embarrassed that his daughter had very nearly caught them in bed together. For that matter, knowing the way she felt about this house, maybe she'd just been incensed by Chelsea's outspoken, negative first impression. He could have reassured her that in Chelsea's present frame of mind, his daughter wouldn't have been impressed if she had walked into an exquisitely furnished palace.

After giving it some thought, Ken decided he liked any of those explanations for Beth's reaction far better than the worrisome possibility that she disliked children. If that was the case, they had a real problem because Chelsea came first with him. He planned to make it up to her for all the turmoil he and her mother had put her through.

He noticed Delores watching him speculatively.

"She didn't expect us, did she?" she guessed. "I don't just mean today. She didn't know about us at all, did she?"

He shook his head.

"Maybe you should go talk to her. Chelsea and I can look around on our own."

"I want Daddy to come with us," his daughter interrupted, her chin set mutinously.

Delores's mouth formed a grim line. "Chelsea Anne Hutchinson, one of these days you are going to have to learn that you can't have everything you want the minute you want it." She plucked the squirming Chelsea from Ken's arms. "Go on. We'll be fine."

He debated doing just that, if only to back up Delores's firm stance with Chelsea, but he figured he owed Beth time to gather her composure. Even knowing his decision was probably based as much on cowardice as consideration, he still shook his head.

"Let's do the tour. I'm sure Beth will join us in a minute."

Delores looked as if she might argue. Finally, she shrugged. "I suppose you know what you're doing," she said, though her tone suggested exactly the opposite.

Ken figured she was probably right to doubt him. He was operating on gut instinct here and something told him there was more behind Beth's unceremonious departure than met the eye, something that would have to be dealt with sooner or later. Not now, though. He wasn't going to do anything to spoil Chelsea's first look at her new home. It was too critical. Beth's questions would have to wait.

Even though he'd set his priorities and was prepared to stand behind them, he felt this terrible weight descending on him. He finally admitted to himself that he had wanted desperately for his daughter and the woman with whom he was becoming involved to like each other. The possibility that Beth might take an instinctive dislike to his child had never occurred to him. And if that's what had happened, he wasn't ready to deal with it just yet.

Chelsea had scrambled out of Delores's arms and stood glaring up at him. "I hate this place," she announced in a petulant tone. "Why do we have to live here?"

Ken barely held on to his already ragged temper. "How can you possibly hate it?" he asked, his tone amazingly even. "You haven't even seen it yet. Let's go up and take a look at your room. It's practically twice the size of the one you've had up till now. You can tell me exactly where you want your bed. The wallpaper we've picked out is supposed to be here on Monday and we can go look for the perfect furniture once you've seen it. This time next week you'll have your room fixed up exactly the way you want it."

He started up the stairs, Delores right behind him. Chelsea lagged behind, but she did follow. Instead of the excited, scampering footsteps he'd envisioned, though, hers were slow and plodding. She refused to come into the room she'd finally chosen from the snapshots he'd taken home. He owed Delores for getting her to do that much. Now, her expression sullen, her lower lip stuck out, she remained in the doorway.

Ken kept his tone deliberately cheerful as he pointed out the already-painted, built-in shelves for her books and dolls, the window seat with its comfortable, brightly covered cushion overlooking the front yard.

"It's ugly," she announced. "And I hate it." Tears welled up in her eyes as she looked up at him pleadingly. "I hate it, Daddy. I hate it. I want to go home."

The tears stripped away his anger and left his emotions raw. He'd never felt more helpless. He gathered her up in his arms.

"Shh, baby. It's going to be okay. You'll see. You just have to give it a chance."

He carried her over to the window seat and sat down. "See, just look outside at all the snow. You'll be able to build a snowman tomorrow. And there's a hill in back. You can go sledding. And you know what

I bought the other day? An old-fashioned sleigh, the kind that has to be drawn by horses."

He noticed the first faint stirring of interest in her still-damp eyes.

"Horses?"

"Right. As soon as the sleigh is all fixed up, I'm going to hire two horses and we'll ride all over the countryside in that sleigh. We'll put jingle bells on the reins. And we'll take along hot chocolate to keep us warm. How does that sound?"

She sniffed, her disdain for everything about this new situation beginning to waver. "Okay, I guess."

"And Thanksgiving is only a week away. We'll have a big turkey dinner with all the trimmings. Maybe your grandmother can stay until then," he suggested with a glance at Delores, who nodded. "And we'll see if Uncle Claude and Aunt Harriet can come up. It'll be just like an old-fashioned Thanksgiving."

"What about Mommy? She'll be all alone in California."

"I'm sure Mommy will have friends to be with on Thanksgiving."

"Why can't she be here with us?"

Ken sighed. "We've been all through that. Remember when we talked about people having dreams about what they want their lives to be like? Being in California is something that Mommy always wanted. She wanted very badly to be an actress. For a very long time she gave up that dream to be with us, but now she really has to try to make it come true. It's not fair for us to ask her to stay here, if she's unhappy."

Chelsea's shattered expression told him she didn't understand her mother's abandonment and that nothing he'd said or could ever say would make her pain go away.

"It doesn't mean she doesn't love you with all her heart," he explained, trying futilely to reassure her. "She just needs to do this for herself right now. One day soon you'll be able to go and visit her. And we'll see Grandma and Grandpa in California, too. It'll be fun, kiddo. You love going to see them, remember?"

He glanced up to see tears in Delores's eyes, tears that she hurriedly brushed away. He pressed a kiss against his daughter's forehead. "In the meantime, can't you try to give this place a chance? I really think you'll like it, if you do."

Her little chest heaved with a sigh of resignation. "Can I have a dog?" she asked with a manipulative air that was all too reminiscent of Pam.

They had never discussed pets before. He hadn't even known Chelsea wanted one. He refused to be rushed into such a decision out of guilt. "We'll talk about it."

"But, Daddy..."

"No argument, Chelsea," he said more harshly than he'd intended. Deliberately injecting a calmer note into his voice, he added, "I said we will talk about it and we will."

"When?" she persisted.

"When the house is completely finished."

Her face fell. "But, Daddy, that will be *forever*."

He shook his head. "No, it won't, pumpkin. We have a miracle worker on our side." At least he hoped they still did. "Let's go downstairs and you can meet her."

"I can hardly wait," Delores murmured just loud enough for him to hear it.

"Watch it or I'll banish you," he taunted her lightly.

"You wouldn't dare, Ken Hutchinson. I know all your deepest, darkest secrets."

"You only think you do."

They were still bantering affectionately when they reached the bottom of the steps just in time to catch Beth trying to slip out the front door.

Pretending he hadn't noticed that anything was amiss, Ken called out too cheerfully, "There you are. We were just talking about you."

She stopped and turned back with painfully obvious reluctance. Her mouth formed a polite smile, but her eyes were desolate. In fact, it looked as if she might have been crying. Guilt sliced through him. The explanations would have to come later, though. There was no time for them now, not with two fascinated onlookers.

"Beth, I'd like you to meet Delores Jensen, the absolute best mother-in-law any man could ever have."

He hadn't thought it possible but even more color seemed to drain out of Beth's complexion. Still, she held out her hand to Delores. "It's very nice to meet you."

"You've done a wonderful job with the house already," Delores told her warmly. "I can see why Ken bought it. Not everyone would see its potential, but I can already imagine how lovely and gracious it will be when it's finished."

Beth's expression softened ever so slightly. "It is an incredible house, isn't it? From the very first time I saw it, I wanted to see a family settled here. Jefferson Grady, the last man who owned it, was eighty-three when he died. He'd lived in it his whole life. I'm afraid, though, that he ran into hard times later in life and he wasn't able to keep it up. His children and grandchildren had all moved away and seldom visited, from what I understand. Every time I drove past, it saddened me to see the house looking so forlorn after years of echoing with children's laughter."

"Well, we're about to change all that, aren't we, Shortstuff?" Ken said, drawing Chelsea over to stand in front of him. "Beth, this is my daughter, Chelsea."

Even though she had to have guessed the relationship, Beth visibly winced at the introduction. "Chelsea, I hope you'll be very happy here," she said, the words mechanical and lacking her usual enthusiasm. She didn't even look at the child as she spoke. As if she'd sensed Beth's displeasure, Chelsea stiffened against the unspoken rejection.

Ken watched the two of them with a sense of despair. How could this warm, gentle woman he'd come to know so intimately suddenly be so cold and distant? And how could she take whatever justifiable anger she might be feeling toward him out on an innocent child? He began to wonder if he knew Beth Callahan nearly as well as he thought he had.

"I really have to go," she said abruptly, still not meeting his gaze.

Even though he could tell it was useless, he tried to argue with her. "Are you sure you can't stay? I'm sure Delores and Chelsea would love to hear about all the plans for the house. Then we could all go to the inn for dinner."

"I have dinner plans," she lied brazenly, obviously fully aware that he knew better. "The samples are all on the desk in your den, if you'd like to show them what we've planned."

"You know I don't know the first thing about all this stuff."

"A couple of weeks ago you might not have, but you're a quick study. Besides, I'm sure you'd like to be alone with your family on their first night in the new house."

The hurt in her voice cut right through him. But before he could argue, she turned and fled, leaving him staring after her openmouthed.

"Seems to me like you've got some fences to mend," Delores said.

"I didn't see any fences," Chelsea chimed in, her expression puzzled.

"Not those kinds of fences," Ken murmured as he listened to Beth's car door slam and the whir of her tires on ice as she sped too quickly away from the house.

Beth cursed a blue streak as she drove away from the Grady place—correction, the *blasted Hutchinson* place. Not once in the handful of meetings they'd had to discuss the house, and certainly not once in all the times they'd lain side by side in her bed, had Ken mentioned a single word about a daughter. Or about the wife that generally came with a child *and* a mother-in-law.

Not that she'd asked, idiot that she was, not even after he'd openly admitted he wouldn't be moving in alone. She hadn't wanted to know the details. She had wanted a few days with him, not an entire future. But somehow, discovering that was all that she would have, changed everything.

She rubbed her hand angrily over her mouth, as if that could take away the lingering sensation of the kisses they'd shared right before her world fell apart. But, she thought hopelessly, if the gesture was a futile attempt to rub out the memory of the kiss, she might as well accept there was nothing on the planet that could strip away all the other sensations they'd shared.

She drew in a deep, determined breath. She just wouldn't accept that. With enough willpower, she could force herself to forget about every single minute they had spent together. Surely there were ways to bury less than two weeks' worth of memories. How indelible could they be?

Perhaps if she thought hard enough about the way Ken had used her, she would want to rip his heart out. At the moment, though, she seemed to be filled with as much self-loathing as fury. How could she ever have fallen for a man who would so blatantly cheat on his wife, a man who had the audacity to introduce his mistress to his mother-in-law and child, for Heaven's sake? Had it been so long since she'd been interested in any man that she'd allowed her judgment to be clouded by physical attraction?

Even if she couldn't wipe out the memories, putting the entire mess behind her would be relatively simple if she never had to see the man again. Unfortunately, she had more rooms to finish in the house. Most of them bedrooms, dammit. And one of them was obviously going to be a little girl's room, which he hadn't mentioned.

To be fair, which she wasn't much inclined to be, they had discussed just one room at a time, starting with the master suite. The subject of what was to be done with those extra bedrooms had never come up. She'd been so caught up in the decor of the master bedroom and her own scandalous imaginings about that king-size bed he'd insisted on that she hadn't given a thought to the possibility that someone else might share it with him.

She lifted her foot off the accelerator and forced herself to slow down and try to treat what had happened this afternoon rationally. First of all, this was a job. She should never once have allowed herself to forget that. Second, he had never mentioned a wife, so maybe she wasn't in the picture. Maybe she was jumping to all the wrong conclusions.

Yeah, right! she thought, chiding herself for the self-delusion. He hadn't mentioned a child, either, and that little girl had definitely called him daddy.

An image of Chelsea came to mind. Beth felt her heart constrict. She was such a beautiful child, her delicate features a softened, more feminine version of her father's. And it had been obvious how much Ken adored her. One tiny part of Beth yearned to be part of such a family, to claim the two of them as her own.

Then she recalled the little girl's derisive remarks about the house, her generally sullen air. Warning bells went off in Beth's head. She knew all about impossible children. It didn't matter that Chelsea had looked like a child right out of the pages of a storybook in her Sunday-best clothes. It only mattered that she was so obviously spoiled by her indulgent family. Her behavior brought too many bitter memories to mind.

Even if the situation weren't impossible, even if there weren't the child's real mother to consider, Beth knew she would never dare to risk involvement in another potentially disastrous relationship. She simply wasn't cut out to be a stepmother, maybe not even a mother. Hadn't she learned that the hard way?

But how had it even gotten this far? Ken might have committed a sin of omission. Her judgment might have failed her. But what about Gillie, her very best friend? Why hadn't Gillie warned her, rather than encouraged her to get involved with Ken? Surely Gillie's fascination with her favorite sports celebrity must have included details on his personal life. She'd known about his charity work, hadn't she? How could she have missed the fact that the man was married and the father of a daughter?

What a mess, she thought with a miserable sigh. Two years of isolation, two years of hard-won contentment, all shattered because she had foolishly dared to believe that she could separate passion and love, and then, when that had been proved wrong, had dared to believe that love was possible for her, after all.

Well, it wouldn't happen again, she resolved. Never again. She even allowed herself to feel some satisfaction over having gathered her composure so quickly, over making the only possible decision given her track record.

By the time she made her way into her house, she was icily calm. Resigned.

Then she went into her bedroom. The sight of her bed, the sheets still rumpled from the previous night's love-making, was her undoing. She sat down on the edge of the bed, drew a pillow into her arms and finally allowed all of the hot, bitter tears of anguish to fall unchecked.

As the emotional storm finally subsided, she was left feeling empty, far emptier than she had been at the end of her marriage to Peter. Because this time she knew, without a single shred of doubt, that this terrible, terrible sense of loss would remain with her for the rest of her life.

Chapter Ten

The next morning, just to get herself back out to the Grady place—the Hutchinson... Oh, forget it, she thought irritably—required a stern lecture on professionalism and so much coffee Beth felt sure she could have single-handedly painted half the quaint little shops on Main Street before the buzz wore off.

She ran nearly a dozen unnecessary errands en route to her job. She lingered over one more cup of coffee at the bakery, evading Lou's worried looks and hoping Gillie would turn up so she could strangle her. She had called her periodically the night before, but hadn't reached her. She would, though. And when she did, the woman was going to get an earful.

When Beth finally gave up on confronting the traitorous Gillie, she headed out of town, driving the rest of the way at a snail's pace, far slower than the road conditions called for. She drove miles out of her way to take a look at a house she was considering taking out an option on for her business. She told herself it was because she'd forgotten to note whether there was an automatic garage door opener. She knew better. She was never slipshod in her note-taking. More important, not one thing in the house had been modernized since much after the turn of the century.

Even when she could prolong the painful meeting with the Hutchinsons no longer, she lingered in her car in front of the house while more minutes ticked away. Lethargy seemed to have stolen her will. She couldn't seem to get herself to budge. The sight of a lopsided snowman wearing a Redskins helmet and an old football jersey didn't help. It was too much of a reminder of what she could expect to find inside—a family, of which she would never be a part.

Finally she was able to convince herself that no matter how long she sat where she was, nothing would change. Ken would still have a family he hadn't mentioned. She would still be heartsick and miserable. And she would still have a job to do. The sooner she got to work, the sooner the house would be finished and the sooner she could begin banishing Ken Hutchinson and his devilishly wicked touches from her mind.

Finally she made her way around back, hoping she could slip into the kitchen unnoticed by anyone except the crew working to enclose in glass the previously screened-in back porch. She waved to them as she opened the door and stepped inside, where she immediately came face-to-face with the person she had most wanted to avoid.

"Good morning," Ken said, his expression determinedly cheerful. "I was worried about you. I thought you'd be here earlier."

"I had things to do."

"And last night? I called several times."

"I was . . . out," she said, stumbling over the lie. In reality, she had unplugged the phone and turned off her answering machine.

Now, standing just a few feet away from him, Beth found she had a hard time clinging to her outrage. For one thing, he didn't seem the least bit guilty. For another, he looked sexy as hell with his cheeks darkened with a faint stubble and his hair rumpled. He was wearing faded jeans and no shirt, despite the fact that the temperature outside had dropped to just above zero the night before. Obviously the heater was very efficient or the man had a metabolism that could have boiled water. She couldn't seem to tear her gaze away from his chest. She wanted—

She stopped her straying thoughts with a sigh. What she wanted she couldn't have.

"Coffee?" he asked, and held up the pot.

Still somewhat taken aback by his cavalier attitude, but determined not to let him see for one instant how he'd hurt her, Beth fell in with his game, whatever it was. She shook her head. "I've already had more than my quota."

"I didn't know it was being rationed."

The quip didn't draw so much as a smile. "Where's your wife?" she inquired bluntly, unable to hold her tongue, after all. "Still in that king-size bed we were about to test yesterday afternoon?"

To her bafflement, he didn't so much as flinch at the sarcasm.

"She's probably on location for some low-budget film by now," he replied without missing a beat. "And, for the record, she's my *ex*-wife."

"Oh." For what seemed like the first time in the past miserable hours, she felt her heart begin to beat again. A tiny ray of hope slipped through her anger.

And then she remembered Chelsea. Wife or no wife, Ken Hutchinson was not the man for her as long as that little girl would be living under his roof. "Are you keeping your daughter, while her mother's working?"

He shook his head, his gray eyes regarding her watchfully. "I have custody."

"Oh," she said again, knowing how dismayed she must sound, but unable to hide her still-raw feelings.

He put down his coffee cup and took a step toward her. Beth backed away and wrapped her coat more tightly around her. He sighed.

"Look, I'm sorry for not telling you I was divorced. I'm sorry I didn't warn you that Chelsea was coming. She and Delores came a day early. I'd planned to tell you last night."

The explanation was too pat to satisfy her thirst for a rip-roaring argument. "There wasn't a single opportunity before that?" she demanded. "Perhaps when we were in bed together?"

Finally, she caught the desired flicker of guilt in his eyes.

"I'm sorry. The subject just never came up. Until just now, I didn't realize you would meet Chelsea and automatically jump to the conclusion that I was still married. That's what put you in such a snit yesterday, isn't it?" He regarded her with obvious regret, then shook his head. "I don't get it. Did you actually think I would carry on an affair with you, knowing that my wife would be arriving any minute? I thought you knew me better than that."

She decided it was best not to respond to that. Instead she said defensively, "I wasn't in a snit."

"Could have fooled me."

Beth glared at him, her temper rising again. "Look, don't you dare try turning me into the villain here. You're the one who—"

"Daddy?"

The frightened voice came from the kitchen doorway. Beth whirled around and took a step back. Chelsea, dressed in denims, a bright red sweater and sneakers, looked as if she were about to cry. Beth locked her hands together to halt the instinctive need to reach out and offer comfort that she knew just as instinctively wouldn't be welcomed.

Ken had no such hesitation. He held out his arms to his daughter. "Come here, Shortstuff. Are you warmer now that you're out of all those wet clothes? I had no idea you were going to manage to stuff as much snow inside your jacket as you got onto that snowman."

Perched in her father's arms, Chelsea kept her gaze fastened on Beth. "Why is she here again?" she demanded rudely.

Ken shot Beth an apologetic look. "I explained that yesterday. She's helping to fix up the house. She'll be around here a lot."

"You said the house would be ready really fast," the little girl said accusingly.

"We've already accomplished a lot," Beth told her, trying not to respond to the child's antagonistic attitude even though she was experiencing this terrible sense of déjà vu.

"Chelsea is anxious to have a dog," Ken explained. "I told her we'd discuss it after the house was finished, which means she'll probably drive the crew and you wild until it's done."

"I see." She forced herself to look directly at the child, while trying just as hard to not see her. If she could only manage to stay on autopilot, maybe none of this would affect her. "What kind of dog do you want?"

"A puppy," Chelsea said curtly.

"Obviously the breed doesn't matter," Ken said.

"I had an Alaskan husky once," Beth said before she could stop herself from making the tiny overture to the child who watched her so warily. "She was beautiful. She had the sweetest temperament you can imagine."

"What's a 'laskan husky?" Chelsea asked suspiciously.

"They're the dogs that pull sleds up in Alaska," Ken explained.

"They're black and white and fluffy," Beth added.

Chelsea seemed intrigued. "They can really pull a sled?"

"Absolutely. They're very strong."

"Maybe Beth will go with us when we look at puppies," Ken suggested.

The change in Chelsea was remarkable. It was as if a switch somewhere inside had been flipped, preventing her from agreeing with anything that included Beth. Scowling at the two adults, she countered, "I want a spotted dog. And I don't need any help choosing."

Ken looked taken aback by his daughter's churlish tone. "We haven't agreed you'll have any dog yet," he reminded her sharply. "And if you speak in that tone of voice again, your chances of getting one will get less and less."

Beth watched as tears of shock and outrage pooled in Chelsea's big gray eyes. Clearly she wasn't used to being reprimanded by her father, something Beth considered to be a very bad sign.

"Maybe you'd better go upstairs and think about that for a while," he said sternly, putting her down.

Chelsea stared up at him for a heartbeat, then turned and ran, her sobs echoing through the house.

Beth watched the entire exchange with mixed feelings. She could practically feel Chelsea's pain at being chastised in front of a stranger, but she also felt an odd sense of relief that Ken, at least, had dealt with her quietly, reasonably and immediately. Maybe he wasn't a father who sent mixed signals to his child as Peter had to Stephanie and Josh. No matter how often Peter had told his children that they were to mind Beth, he undermined her decisions at every turn.

She could hear murmured words from upstairs and assumed Delores Jensen was consoling her granddaughter. She couldn't help wondering whether the older woman would provide the leniency that Ken had not in an attempt to make up for the absence of Chelsea's mother. If so, Beth saw little chance for improvement in Chelsea's belligerent behavior.

She reminded herself it was not her problem. She was here to work on the house, not to offer childrearing theories. She hardly had the expertise for that, she conceded wryly.

Forcing herself to concentrate on the job, she finally removed her coat and edged toward the doorway, hoping to make a quick escape into Ken's den where all the materials and plans had been stored.

"Beth?"

Ken's quiet tone stopped her. She glanced up at him and saw that he was regarding her with a puzzled expression. "I will make this misunderstanding up to you. I promise."

"It doesn't matter," she said. Even to her own ears she sounded unconvincing.

"It does matter," he insisted. "I want you and Chelsea to be friends. I would hate it if it were my fault that you can't be."

Beth drew in a deep breath and tried to squelch the temptation that raced through her. She couldn't—she *wouldn't*—put herself in such a vulnerable position again. It had been too painful the first time.

"I think maybe we'd better clear something up," she said firmly. "You hired me to do a job here. When it's done, I'll be out of your way." She leveled her gaze straight at him and tried to keep her voice just as steady. "As for anything else that went on between us, it was never meant to last."

She saw his eyes widen with shock, but she was too anxious to get away to someplace where she could quiet her own trembling to worry about his reaction. She'd made it no more than half a dozen steps when she felt his hand close around her arm. The next thing she knew she was being spun around until she was crushed against his bare chest, the wind practically knocked out of her.

"How can you say that?" he demanded harshly, his gray eyes stormy. "You know what we've shared the past couple of weeks was more than some casual fling."

Forcing her voice to remain cool, she said, "Maybe for you. Not for me."

She had thought the comment would fill him with indignation or disgust. She had been sure he would release her then. Instead his grip tightened and he studied her even more intently. That slow examination made her increasingly nervous, increasingly worried that she would give away her own tumultuous feelings.

"You're deliberately lying to me," he said with quiet certainty. "What I don't understand is why."

She managed a shrug. "You can believe whatever you like, if that protects your ego. It won't change the truth."

She caught the flicker of anger barely an instant before his mouth came crushing down on hers. It didn't give her nearly enough warning. The hard, punishing kiss practically knocked the breath out of her. There was no mistaking its intent, either. Ken was determined to make a liar out of her.

Beth was equally determined that he wouldn't succeed. She didn't struggle against the sensual assault. She didn't do anything. She kept her mind focused on a list of chores she needed to do and willed her body to remain limp. Trying to stay oblivious to that kiss was the hardest thing she'd ever had to do, but she did it, and a small measure of triumph early on kept her strong enough to continue resisting.

After a few interminable seconds, Ken finally pulled away, looking shaken and confused by her total lack of response.

Beth bit her lip to keep it from trembling and prayed the tears she could feel gathering wouldn't betray her by spilling down her cheeks before she could get away.

"Are you satisfied?" she asked quietly.

His jaw set, he glowered at her. "Oh, no. I am far from satisfied. You can run from me now, if you like, but I will get to the bottom of this. Count on it."

Beth didn't give him a chance to change his mind. She raced toward the den, slamming the door behind her and leaning against it as the tears cascaded down her cheeks. How in God's name was she going to survive several more weeks of this? How long would it be before she betrayed herself by melting beneath one of his kisses? How long could she hide the way she trembled at his touch?

He thought she was only lying to him, when the truth of it was that she was lying even more desperately to herself. She had spent an entire night telling herself she didn't care one whit for this man, when a few seconds in his arms was all it had taken to prove otherwise.

In an act of sheer desperation, she gathered what she needed to do her work for the day and raced for the door. "I'll be working at home if you need me," she hollered to the crew as she passed.

She tossed the invoices and samples into the back of the car, then got behind the wheel. Just as she was ready to pull away, she glanced up at the house. Two pairs of gray eyes watched her. Chelsea's round little face was pressed against the window upstairs. Ken's far more disturbing gaze met hers from the living room window. She could practically hear him calling her a coward, even though his lips never moved.

So what, she tossed back at him mentally. Better to be a coward in this situation than to expose her vulnerabilities. It had taken two long years to begin to feel some measure of self-confidence. She wouldn't let anyone ever shatter that again.

It took every ounce of self-restraint Ken possessed to keep from running out of the house after Beth. He watched her frantic departure with a sense of absolute frustration and outrage.

Dammit, he'd made a mistake. He hadn't committed a felony. There was something going on with her that he clearly didn't understand. He had a feeling it went far beyond any shock she might have felt over discovering he was a divorced, single parent. Unfortunately, that role was all too common these days.

When he had held Beth just now, when he had kissed her, she had stiffened as if he were a stranger. He knew with everything in him how much that effort to remain aloof must have cost her. She had been far too responsive a mere twenty-four hours earlier to be so icily cold now without really working at it. That wasn't ego talking. That was basic human anatomy. What he didn't have a clue about was why she had felt that was necessary.

He looked up at a sound in the foyer. Chelsea had crept down the stairs and stood watching him, an oddly satisfied expression on her face. He wasn't sure he wanted to know what that look was all about.

"I'm sorry, Daddy," she said, clinging to her favorite doll.

He regarded her skeptically. "Really?"

She nodded, her expression solemn. "I promise I'll be really good. Can I stay down here with you?"

He sighed at the plaintive note in her voice. How could he possibly stay mad at her? "Where's your grandmother?"

"Hanging up my clothes."

"Shouldn't you be up there helping her?"

"She says I just get in the way."

Ken doubted Delores had said any such thing. If anything, he suspected Chelsea had learned that expression from Pam. He had planned to try to put in a couple of hours working, but after reading the forlorn expression on his daughter's face he abandoned that plan.

"Run up and get your grandmother. We'll go for a ride so you can see the town. Tell her we'll stop somewhere for lunch."

A smile spread across Chelsea's face. "And we can look for a puppy."

"Drop that for now," he warned gently.

Her grin didn't waver. "We'll see," she said blithely.

She said it in that adult way that often took him totally by surprise. She was definitely Pam's daughter, all right. Somehow he couldn't find much comfort in that.

"Bundle up," he called after her.

He put on a shirt then grabbed his own jacket and scarf from the back of a chair and tugged on a pair of boots. "I'll be outside warming up the car," he shouted. "Don't be long."

"We're hurrying, Daddy. We'll be there really fast."

Outside as he sat shivering in the icy car, Ken wondered if he dared take them by Beth's house. Perhaps they could persuade her to join them. Then he thought of the possibility she would refuse and decided now was not the time for Chelsea to suffer another rejection. Maybe it was better if they made this strictly a family outing, he conceded, trying to ignore the sense of disappointment the decision sent through him.

The roads had been plowed and sanded since the previous day, making the drive relatively easy. As they passed the house he had learned belonged to Roger Killington, the tactless, but well-intentioned bank president, Chelsea apparently caught sight of a sign he hadn't even noticed before.

"Daddy, doesn't that sign on the tree say Puppies?"

He groaned and wished for an instant that his daughter's spelling skills weren't quite so advanced. "Yep. Very good," he said, and kept right on driving. He caught Delores's smirk. "Don't say it."

"Did you hear a word from me?" she remarked agreeably. "I'm just along for the ride."

By the time they reached town, it was almost noon. The shops along Berry Ridge's main street were about as busy as they ever got. It was too cold to linger on the sidewalk chatting, so most people ducked into the stores when they ran into neighbors. Most places kept a couple of chairs around for these impromptu visits.

Feeling surprisingly at home, Ken pointed out the general store, a gallery of local arts and crafts, an old-fashioned candy store and ice-cream parlor, a model train shop, a combination bookstore and card shop, and the bakery.

"Where's the toy store?" Chelsea demanded.

Knowing she was referring to the kind of superstore that he hated, he gave her a sympathetic look. "Sorry. The closest big store like that is twenty miles away. But several of these stores have toys."

"I'll bet they don't have electronic games," she said derisively. "And I'll bet they don't have Barbie."

"I guess you won't be wanting to look around, then," he said. "We might as well go have lunch."

Chelsea started to argue, then fell silent. Ken had planned to make the twenty-mile drive to the nearest fast-food outlet, but just then he spotted Beth's car half a block from the bakery and guessed she was there having lunch. When a space by the curb opened up just in front of him, he pulled in.

Chelsea shot him an appalled look. "I want a hamburger."

"You can have one."

"But where? I don't see McDonald's."

"Sorry, kiddo. You'll have to make do with the kind they have here," he said, leading the way toward the bakery.

They were almost to the door when he felt Delores's hand on his arm.

"Are you sure this is such a good idea?" she asked.

"What?"

"I'm not blind, young man. I saw her car. I also heard the two of you arguing this morning. This doesn't strike me as the place to try making up. Word will be all over town by nightfall."

Ken recognized there was some truth in that, but he was determined to try to normalize things between himself and Beth, no matter what it took. He also wanted her to spend some time with Chelsea. Perhaps here, in public, there would be the kind of buffer that would ease the situation.

"It'll be fine," he reassured Delores.

She muttered something that sounded like "Men," and rolled her eyes.

The bakery wasn't all that large, but at the moment it was crowded. It took him a minute to spot Beth in the booth at the back, sitting all alone and looking every bit as dejected as he'd been feeling. Plastering a smile on his face, he determinedly headed her way. He was already shrugging out of his jacket.

"Hi," he said cheerfully as he approached the table.

Her head snapped up. "What are you doing here?"

"We came to have lunch. Mind if we join you? All the other tables are taken," he said, not waiting for a reply before nudging his way onto the seat beside her.

Temper flared in her eyes, but she gave a reluctant nod, probably because she caught the sympathetic expression on his ex-mother-in-law's face.

Once they were all settled, Lou came over to take their order, her observant gaze pinned mostly on Beth. "You want me to hold that order of chowder for you until their food is ready?"

Beth was silent for so long Ken guessed she was warring with herself between politeness and a desire to flee as quickly as possible.

"I'll wait," she finally said with an air of resignation.

With the ordering out of the way and his immediate tactical goal accomplished, Ken was suddenly at a loss about how to proceed. Fortunately, Delores smoothed the way by commenting on the plans for the house. In no time the two women were caught up in a discussion of the appliances needed for the kitchen. Ken listened happily, certain that this was the first step toward a permanent thaw.

Chelsea, unfortunately, was clearly bored by it all. As the talk of refrigerators and stoves and washers and dryers went on, he watched her expression grow increasingly sullen. She picked up her fork and tapped it again and again against the Formica-topped table.

"Stop that, sweetie. We're trying to have a conversation," Delores said.

When that didn't work, she forcibly removed the fork from Chelsea's tight fist and without missing a beat went right on discussing the merits of trash compactors. Ken watched the incident with admiration.

Then, in an action as unexpected as it was sudden, Chelsea hit her glass of cola and sent it streaming straight toward Beth. The sticky, dark liquid splashed over Beth's clothes and into her face. Ken didn't have a doubt in his mind that Chelsea had sent the glass flying deliberately. Neither, if the expression on her face was any indication, did Beth.

Lou came rushing over with a washcloth, which she handed Beth, and a towel she used to mop up the rest of the spill, clucking all the while. "Accidents happen around here all the time," she said briskly. Her kindly gaze fell on Chelsea. "Don't you worry about it. I'll bring you another drink."

"I don't think that will be necessary," Ken said. "I don't believe Chelsea really wanted that one." He met his daughter's gaze. "Did you?"

Her lower lip trembled.

"You might tell Beth that you're sorry," he said more gently when Lou had gone.

She shook her head.

"Chelsea!"

She finally lifted her head and looked at Beth. "I didn't mean it."

"I'm sure you didn't," Beth said quietly.

The comment was gracious, but Ken knew without a doubt that she didn't believe what she was saying.

She and Chelsea watched each other as warily as a couple of enemy warlords meeting for the first time.

Ken suddenly felt like the negotiator who'd forced a meeting and now anticipated being shot...probably twice.

Chapter Eleven

After an endless weekend during which she'd had plenty of time to contemplate Chelsea's deliberate spilling of her soft drink, Beth forced herself to go back to Ken's house. The only way she was going to survive this ordeal was by taking it one day at a time, one hour at a time. She felt as if she were in a recovery program. In those, however, a person was advised to avoid all contact with the troublesome substance. She was going to have to face her demon every single day and try to emerge from the meetings emotionally unscathed.

For the first time since the work had begun, she felt it necessary to ring the doorbell when she arrived. Delores, not Ken, greeted her, which settled her nerves somewhat. Then Delores added that Ken had gone out for the morning to take care of some business. The only thing that might have filled her with a greater sense of relief would have been the news that Chelsea had gone with him. Unfortunately, the little girl was standing right beside her grandmother, her expression solemn and distrustful.

"Chelsea and I are going to bake some cookies. Would you like some when we're through?" Delores asked.

"I'd love some," Beth said, keeping her gaze on Delores so she wouldn't have to deal with all of the conflicting emotions Ken's daughter stirred in her.

"With tea or coffee?"

"I'd love a cup of coffee, but don't go to any extra trouble."

"It's no trouble. I brewed a big pot this morning. I can't wake up without it. And when this one gets going," Delores said, smoothing Chelsea's blond hair, "I need to be fully alert."

"My grandmother bakes the very best cookies in the whole world," Chelsea volunteered, startling Beth with the friendly overture. For once there seemed to be no guile in her eyes, no resentment, just a sparkling anticipation of the morning's planned activity.

"I'll bet she does," Beth said, smiling at the childish enthusiasm despite herself. "What kind are your favorites?"

"Chocolate chip. But pretty soon we're going to bake Christmas cookies with red icing and sprinkles." Her expression suddenly turned belligerent. "Just like we did at my real house last year," she said as if to emphasize that this house would never be accepted as her real home.

Delores sent Beth an apologetic look. "She'll adapt before you know it," she said.

Beth shook her head. "Not necessarily," she said.

Apparently something in her voice conveyed far more meaning than the words alone, because Delores gave her a penetrating look. Before she could explore the remark, though, Chelsea tugged on her hand.

"Let's go, Grandma. I want to have lots and lots of cookies for Daddy when he gets home."

"In a minute," Delores began, but Chelsea's expression turned mutinous.

"Now," she insisted, earning a warning glance from her grandmother that effectively silenced her. She retaliated for the rebuke by glaring at Beth.

Delores sighed and gave Beth a look that was full of regret. "We'll talk more later," she said to Beth, obviously intent on keeping peace.

It was a tactic that Beth could have told her wouldn't work in the long run. Instead, wishing that the warm, older woman could become a friend, Beth simply nodded. She had recognized at once that they would never have the chance, if Chelsea had her way. The child seemed ready to do everything in her power to make sure that Beth remained a safe distance from everyone in her family.

As Beth went into Ken's office and tried to get to work, she reminded herself that a seven-year-old who had just been through a traumatic divorce probably needed reassurance that those still around her wouldn't be taken away. Emotionally, she probably required all the extra attention, especially in a new place where she had yet to meet friends. It was probably to be expected that she would view any stranger as a threat.

The generous, caring, rational side of Beth could accept all of the time-honored psychological explanations for Chelsea's behavior. The vulnerable, fragile part of her was terrified to open her heart to yet another child who seemed intent on rejecting her love.

Seated behind Ken's desk, she went over another batch of invoices, comparing them to the prices she'd originally been quoted and to the shipments stacked across the room. As she was shuffling papers, she found a note from Ken asking if there was any way possible the wallpapering in the dining room could be completed by Thanksgiving. He'd promised Chelsea an old-fashioned meal at home and didn't want to disappoint her.

Beth thought of her own plans for the holiday. She'd been invited to Gillie's, as usual, and to the Killingtons' for their annual celebration for family and business associates. Given her present mood, she would be wise to turn them both down. She wasn't fit company for anyone. She couldn't help wondering if she would have felt that way if Ken had asked her to join them for Thanksgiving dinner.

Releasing a sigh, she picked up the phone and called the wallpaper hangers and made arrangements with the owner, Steve Wilcox, to come in on Tuesday to do the dining room as a rush order. The other rooms would be done the following week.

"You'll have that place finished in time for Christmas," he promised.

"Thanks, Steve. You're an angel. Anything you can do to speed things along would be greatly appreciated."

"Remember that the next time I ask you out," he teased.

The man was gorgeous in an offbeat, artsy sort of way, with his thick brown hair drawn back in a ponytail and his chiseled features. He was also funny and hard-working. But he was barely twenty-five, for goodness' sake. At the moment she felt about a hundred years older. "You know perfectly well I'm too old for you."

"That's your opinion, not mine."

She laughed. "You are good for my ego, I'll give you that."

"Oh, my, I've scored two points in one morning. I'd better quit while I'm ahead. Add 'em to my score."

"I wasn't aware we were keeping score."

"I am. I figure there's probably some magical number I'll eventually accumulate and you'll break down and say yes."

"Isn't there some lovely young woman your own age you'd rather go out with?"

"I haven't met a woman in the entire state of Vermont who can hold a candle to you."

"Ah, Steve, you have definitely mastered the fine art of flattery. You're making my head spin."

"That's the idea," he said. "See you in the morning. Eight sharp. You bring the coffee. I'll work on my seduction technique."

"It's a deal," she said, smiling to herself as she hung up.

"Who's the admirer?" Ken said.

Beth's head snapped up. He was leaning against the doorjamb, his posture lazy. His eyes, however, had a dangerous, predatory gleam in them. "I didn't know you were back."

"I got here just in time to hear you tell some man he was making your head spin."

He sounded downright disgruntled about it, too, she thought with a tiny glimmer of satisfaction. "That was Steve Wilcox. You'll meet him tomorrow. He's the man I hired to hang your wallpaper. He'll have the dining room all set for Thanksgiving."

"Thanks," he said automatically. "I thought it was the plumber I had to worry about."

"All of the guys are buddies."

"Buddies?" he said doubtfully.

She shrugged. "Why not? It is possible for men and women to be friends."

"I suppose."

"Planning a big gathering for Thanksgiving?" she asked, hoping to get off the subject of her social life before he discovered how studiously she had avoided having one up until she'd met him.

"Delores, Chelsea, two close friends from D.C." He paused and waited until her gaze met his. "And you, if you don't already have other plans."

"I've been invited to two parties that day," she said hurriedly, hoping to evade temptation.

He watched her closely. "You said invited. You didn't say you'd accepted the invitations."

"No," she agreed, wishing the man didn't have the perceptiveness of an expert psychic. "But if I go anywhere, I should accept one of those."

"Because they asked first?"

She shrugged. "That's what Miss Manners would advise."

"You're not just using that to avoid joining us?"

"Why would I do that?"

"Because you're suddenly uncomfortable in this house," he said, straightening. He walked slowly across the room, then perched on the corner of the desk so his thigh was brushing hers. "I can't tell you how much I regret that."

Even though she knew what was smart, even though she recognized that an honest answer had danger written all over it, she couldn't help admitting, "Me, too."

"Then come for dinner," he repeated persuasively. "You'll really like Claude Dobbins and his wife. They're good people. Delores takes full credit for their marriage. Claude was a confirmed bachelor and Harriet was one very unhappy lady until Delores took charge. They're expecting a baby in the spring."

"They sound really special."

"They are. Claude's my best friend. He'd do anything in the world for me, Delores and Chelsea. It goes both ways."

"It must be nice to have friends like that," she said, thinking of her own best friend, who'd let her walk right into this hornet's nest with a single father even though Gillie knew her background. Gillie had been mysteriously elusive the past few days. Perhaps she'd gotten wind of how things were going between Beth and Ken and had decided to lay low.

"Then you have to meet them," Ken insisted. "I know Delores would love to have you join us. She thinks you're terrific."

She shook her head. "It's too awkward."

"Awkward how?"

"Me, your ex-mother-in-law, your friends," she said, carefully avoiding any mention of the real problem—Chelsea. "Thanksgiving should be for family and friends. I'm an outsider."

"Not with me. And you won't be with them, if you'll give them a chance."

The invitation tempted like the lure of lemonade on a summer day. She resisted. "I can't."

"It's Chelsea, isn't it? She's the real problem."

"I never said that," she said, shocked that he'd zeroed in on it. Even though she credited him with amazing sensitivity, she had assumed he would be blind to anything having to do with his daughter.

"Look, I know she hasn't behaved very well toward you. Don't take it personally, though. She's been difficult for all of us to handle. She threw a tantrum with Claude the other day and she adores him. And I can't tell you the battles she and I have had over this move."

"You can't blame her," she said. "She's been through a lot of changes."

"That doesn't entitle her to behave like a spoiled brat," he said, his expression grim. "I'm not trying to excuse her behavior, but can't you make some allowances for what she's going through?"

"Of course I can." From a nice, objective perspective she actually agreed with what he was saying. Unfortunately she wasn't able to be objective in this situation. Still, because it was the expected reply from an adult, she said, "I understand exactly the kind of turmoil she's experiencing."

Ken's gaze narrowed. "Did you grow up in a broken home?"

"No. I've just done a lot of reading on children who've lost parents through death or divorce."

"Any particular reason?"

Beth wasn't ready to get into her past with him. The present was complicated enough. "Just a topic that fascinated me."

"I see," he said, though it was clear that he didn't.

He sighed and Beth felt certain he'd resigned himself to accepting her decision. Instead he reached over and cupped her face between his hands. Then, while her heart began to thump unsteadily, he slowly leaned down and touched his lips to hers. The heat was there and gone before she could savor its warmth. Just as she was about to utter an agonized plea, his mouth closed over hers again, this time with all of the hunger and persuasiveness at his command.

Beth melted. Her resistance toppled. The only thing in her head was the need to be next to the source of the exquisite heat that made her blood flow like warm honey. When the kiss finally ended, Ken ran his thumb over her swollen lips and kept his unrelenting gaze pinned on hers.

"Say yes," he said softly.

"You don't play fair," she murmured.

A smile tugged at his lips. "I've told you before, I'll do whatever it takes to get what I want. Right now, what I want is for you to come here for Thanksgiving dinner on Thursday. I want you with me on the first holiday I celebrate in this house. This isn't some whim. It matters to me, Beth."

The words weakened her already shaky defenses. And with Ken's vital nearness consuming all of her thoughts, Beth could barely remember why she'd been hesitant in the first place.

"I'll come," she said finally. "But only if Delores will let me help."

"You'll have to negotiate that part of the deal with her," he said, looking satisfied at the relatively easy victory. "I have what I want," he murmured just before his mouth settled on hers one more time.

After he'd met Steve Wilcox on Tuesday, Ken couldn't believe he had even for a single instant been jealous of the man when he'd overheard Beth on the phone with him. It was obvious the two of them had a friendly, teasing rapport, but he was too young, too laid-back for a woman like Beth.

Still, it had disconcerted him to see her chatting so easily with the other man, touching Steve so casually and with such affection, when it seemed she was doing everything in her power to avoid intimacy with him. The entire experience had rankled until he finally convinced himself that he would be able to find some occasion on Thanksgiving to get her alone for a long, quiet talk...and more, if she'd let him anywhere near her. His entire body ached every time he thought about what they'd shared for a few short days before Chelsea and Delores had unexpectedly turned up that afternoon a week earlier.

Thanksgiving morning dawned with bright blue skies. He expected Claude and Harriet sometime around eleven. They were taking a crack-of-dawn flight from D.C. to Hartford, then renting a car for the two-hour drive to Berry Ridge. Chelsea had been on pins and needles since dawn awaiting their arrival.

"You'd think it had been months instead of days since you'd seen them," Ken said as she ran back and forth between the kitchen where the turkey was in the oven and the living room windows.

"But I really, really miss them," she informed him.

Ken sighed. "I know you do, baby."

She scowled. Before she could say a word, he grinned. "I know, you're not a baby."

"I'm not, Daddy. I'm getting all growed up."

"In that case, I want to talk to you about something. Come over here."

Chelsea approached him cautiously.

"Up here," he said, indicating his lap. "You're not too big for that, are you?"

"No."

She threw her arms around his neck and hugged him, as if to prove it. For an instant he allowed himself to recall what a wonderful, sweet-tempered, snuggly baby she had been. If only they could recapture those untroubled days when Chelsea had felt secure and hadn't needed to be constantly testing the limits of his love.

He regarded her seriously. "Now, then, I want to ask you for a really big favor today. I want you to try really, really hard to be extra nice to Beth." Chelsea's instantly mutinous scowl dismayed him.

"I don't like her," she said at once.

"You barely know her."

"I don't like her," Chelsea said stubbornly.

Ken fought to hang on to his patience. "Why not?"

As he'd suspected, she had no ready answer for that. Her brow knit in concentration and a frown settled on her lips. "Because," she said, apparently hoping the all-encompassing remark would be answer enough.

Ken wasn't about to settle for it. "No, you don't. If you really don't like Beth, I'd like to understand why."

"Because, Daddy, I don't think she likes me."

"That's not true," he said automatically, even though he had no way of knowing if Chelsea might be right. After all, she hadn't made herself very likable. And he had detected Beth's restraint himself. "I'm sure she would love you if she got to know you. You just haven't given her much of a chance. Since you're growing up now, I thought maybe you could try just a little harder."

She frowned. "You're not going to marry her, are you?"

The question took Ken totally by surprise. Not because he hadn't wondered the same thing himself, but because Chelsea had. Out of the mouths of babes, he thought wryly.

"I don't know," he told her honestly.

"I don't want you to," Chelsea said firmly. "I already have a mommy."

"I know you do, Shortstuff. And even if I do decide to get married again one of these days to Beth or anyone else, no one will ever try to take the place of your mommy."

"Are you sure? My friend Kevin has a stepmother and he says she's really mean when he goes to visit. She won't let him do anything. She says she might not be his mother, but she's still in charge when he's in her house."

Ken winced as he considered the problems that family must have. He prayed he could find some way to avoid them. Maybe Harriet, who probably dealt with troubled kids from broken homes every day, would have some advice for him.

"Well, I would never, ever marry someone who would be mean to you," he said for now. "I promise. Okay?" He tugged on the braid Delores had plaited for Chelsea that morning. "Do we have a deal?"

"Deal," Chelsea said, and held up her hand for a high five.

She scrambled down. "You watch for Uncle Claude and Aunt Harriet, okay? I've got to go see if the turkey's done yet."

"If you keep opening that oven door, it will never get done," he warned.

"I don't open it," she shouted back. "I peek through the little window, just like Grandma does."

No sooner had Chelsea scampered off, than Delores turned the corner and came into the living room.

"Eavesdropping?" he asked. Actually he was hoping she had heard. Maybe then she could offer her own insights into the awkwardness between Beth and Chelsea.

"I was on my way in when I heard the two of you talking. I didn't want to interrupt."

"But you didn't budge, either, did you?"

Ignoring the remark, she settled on the sofa opposite him. "You evaded Chelsea's question about your feelings for Beth," she accused.

"I didn't have an answer for her."

"I think you do. I think maybe you were just afraid she wouldn't like it."

He scowled at his meddling and unfortunately too perceptive ex-mother-in-law. He'd wanted her to talk about Beth and Chelsea, not him. He should have known that would be impossible. "Okay, I didn't want to get her all worked up over something that might never happen. She's not ready to hear my plans." He grinned ruefully. "Unfortunately, neither is Beth. She's turned skittish all of a sudden."

He dropped the light note and looked at Delores. "You've seen Chelsea and Beth together. Do you think Chelsea could be right? Does Beth dislike her?"

Delores slowly shook her head, her expression thoughtful. "I think it's more like she's afraid of her."

"Afraid? Chelsea's a seven-year-old child."

"With the power to come between the two of you," Delores reminded him. "Give some thought to that. I'm going to make sure your daughter hasn't crawled into the oven with the turkey."

Ken might have dismissed Delores's theory without further thought if he hadn't seen yet more evidence of

Beth's wariness around his child practically the minute she walked through the door.

She had just stepped into the foyer when Chelsea came racing out of the kitchen shouting for her Uncle Claude and Aunt Harriet. At the sight of Beth, she skidded to a stop, disappointment written all over her face. Beth's smile, in turn, faded, her expression transformed in a heartbeat to uncertainty.

Ken tried to smooth over the moment by explaining that his daughter had been watching for the other guests practically since dawn. Before he could say much, though, the couple in question pulled up outside and Chelsea was racing down the front walk where she was caught up in Claude's beefy arms and swung high in the air. She squealed with delight.

Ken glanced at Beth. She was watching the scene with an unreadable expression. Not until he looked into her eyes could he interpret what she was thinking. The desolation he saw there, though, very nearly broke his heart.

Although he'd been about to follow Chelsea down the walk, instead he stayed where he was and took Beth's icy hand in his own. She glanced at him, clearly startled by the gesture.

"We're going to work this out," he promised her, even though he wasn't entirely sure what needed to be resolved. He just knew that the woman standing beside him desperately needed reassurance of some kind.

To his dismay, though, his promise didn't seem to give her any comfort at all. Without a word, she slowly and deliberately withdrew her hand from his.

"I'll go see what I can do to help Delores." With that she turned and fled, leaving him more confused—and lonely—than he'd ever been in his entire life.

Chapter Twelve

Beth wasn't sure what she'd been expecting, but it hadn't been the giant of a man that Claude Dobbins turned out to be. The man had to weigh in at three hundred pounds and he looked to be solid as a rock and mean as an urban street fighter.

Until he smiled, which he did a lot. Then his entire demeanor turned from fierce as a lion to gentle as a lamb. The transformation was astonishing. Beth found herself warming to him immediately, especially when she saw the way he treated Chelsea and Delores, sweeping them up in exuberant bear hugs and tickling them until they were both helpless with laughter.

"No, Uncle Claude! No!" Chelsea squealed, her fair complexion, blond hair and petite frame a stark contrast to the huge, ebony man who was teasing her.

"You scared of me, Half-pint?"

"No," she protested, flinging her arms around his thick neck. "I love you."

"Ditto," he said. "Now why don't you tell me what you and your daddy have been doing since you snuck off to the wilderness."

"Don't you go pumping my daughter for information," Ken warned him, his expression filled with tolerant amusement. "That's a low-down, sneaky tactic."

"So what else is new?" Harriet asked, shooting Beth a commiserating glance. "Girl, I hope you have an endless amount of patience, because when these two get together, they are one demanding handful. You can't believe half of what they're saying. I'm thinking of hiring one of those NFL referees during the off-season just to keep Claude in line."

"What makes you think one of those guys can control him any better off the field than on?" Ken said. He launched into a litany of exploits that had confounded the officials and the opposing teams.

"Exaggerations," Claude retorted. "You're making that up, my man."

"Well, what about..." Ken began, describing another incident and then another.

While the others hooted at Claude's increasingly indignant expression, Beth studied his wife. Harriet Dobbins was as much of a surprise as her husband had been. She was tall—at least six feet—and thin, with the regal bearing of someone who'd been made to go through adolescence with a book balanced on her head. Someone had taught her pride and grace, traits not always associated with such height in a woman.

And, like her husband, she had a natural, all-encompassing warmth. Beth instantly felt as if she'd known her for years.

Then Claude turned that smile of his on Beth. Brown eyes examined her thoroughly, then gleamed with approval. "Yes, indeed," he said to Ken. "I can see why you'd be willing to freeze your butt off up here."

"Claude!" Harriet chided as she might a wayward child. She shot an apologetic glance toward Beth.

He rolled his eyes. "Pardon me, Beth. My wife thinks I have no couth whatsoever."

"It must come from spending most of your life bulldozing over men on a football field," Harriet shot back. She grinned at Beth. "Getting paid for his brawn instead of his brain has ruined him for civilized company. You'd never guess this man has a near genius IQ."

Claude scooped his wife up as if she were weightless. "This brawn is what keeps you in champagne and caviar, my dear."

"Put me down, you oaf. You haven't bought me any champagne since our honeymoon." She turned a helpless gaze on Delores. "I hope you're proud of yourself for getting me married to this man."

Delores shrugged, looking unrepentant. "Must be happy enough," she observed. "There's a baby on the way."

Chelsea's eyes widened. "A baby? When? Can I play with her?"

"It's going to be a boy," Claude informed her huffily. "And he won't be playing no sissy girls' games, so you just get that idea right out of your head, young lady.''

"Claude is not familiar with the concept of woman's lib," Harriet said dryly. "Boys play football. Girls get dolls. There will be no muddying of the water in his family."

"Do you know for a fact it's going to be a boy?" Ken chimed in. "Or is that wishful thinking on Claude's part?"

"The man hasn't figured out that he can't just stand around telling my belly to produce a boy," Harriet said, regarding her husband with obvious affection. "Me, I'm hoping for a girl, just to spite him. Besides, I think it would be kind of nice to see how he handles the boys who come to date his precious firstborn. Or what he does when his daughter decides to go to court to be allowed to play high school football."

All of the talk of babies and families was beginning to take its toll on Beth. She glanced at Ken and saw that he was watching her, his expression thoughtful. A slow smile spread across his face. He came to sit beside her. "Getting ideas?"

"About what?" she asked.

"Babies."

"Not me," she said so adamantly that Ken's expression immediately shifted to a puzzled frown.

"Why not? I'll bet you'd make a wonderful mother."

The well-meant compliment brought the immediate sting of tears. Beth jumped up as if she'd touched a live wire. "I think I'll go check on dinner."

"Beth?"

She caught his worried expression and looked away. "I'll be right back."

In the kitchen, she stood with her hands braced on the counter and battled the tears welling up in her eyes. Memories of other holidays that had never lived up to expectations came spilling back.

She had tried. Oh, how she had tried to make things special for the years she had been with Peter, Josh and Stephanie. She had worked for days to prepare gourmet meals and for weeks before to make sure the house was filled with the right decorations, the right flowers, the right evocative scents or the right gifts.

Not once in all that time had she ever received a word of thanks, not even from her husband. Peter had taken the efforts for granted. The children had been deliberately disinterested in anything she had to offer, even when she had shopped all over town to give them an impossible-to-find present she knew they had wanted. From them she received only disdain.

Even the perfect gift always had some flaw. The color was wrong, or it had an almost-impossible-to-see scratch, or it was what they had wanted last week, but not this. Even the tastiest meal could have been seasoned a little differently. And nothing—*nothing*—was ever as their mother had done it and therefore wasn't worthy of their appreciation or even their simple courtesy.

The terrible thing about today was not how much it resembled all those other disasters, but how wonderfully close it was to the way she'd always imagined a family holiday should be, filled with laughter and shared memories. It was a bittersweet sample of the one thing she would never have on a permanent basis, not with Ken Hutchinson at any rate.

She heard the kitchen door swing open and surreptitiously dried her eyes. If Ken noticed the tears, he pretended otherwise.

"How's the turkey?" he asked, though it was obvious from the concern written all over his face that he was far more worried about her than he was about dinner.

"I was just about to check," she said, and hurriedly did just that. "Looks done to me. Is there a fork around to test it?"

Ken handed one to her.

"Perfect," she said.

He nudged her aside with his hip in a casual gesture that seemed somehow very familiar and very right.

"Let me take it out, so it can cool a bit," he said. "Is there a place for it on the counter?"

Beth saw that Delores had put a thick wooden cutting board next to the already-baked pumpkins pies. "I think the roasting pan can sit right here," she said.

The huge turkey was a golden brown. As soon as the pan was safely on the counter, Ken snitched a piece of white meat and handed it to Beth, then reached for another sample for himself.

"I saw that," Delores said as she came in to join them.

Within minutes, everyone was crowded into the kitchen as side dishes were prepared or popped into the oven for warming. Chelsea was underfoot, trying to sneak a taste of everything. For once she didn't say anything overtly antagonistic toward Beth. In fact, for the most part, she just ignored her. That only hurt when Beth stopped to consider how sweetly the child was behaving toward everyone else.

Thanksgiving dinner was a huge success. Compliments flew, from praise of the food that Beth had brought to Delores's perfectly baked turkey and mashed potatoes and on to Chelsea's neatly colored decorations for the table. The table groaned under the weight of all the dishes, which contained more than enough for a gathering twice this size.

As they ate, Beth felt Ken's gaze returning to her time and again, his expression speculative, as if he couldn't understand why a woman who rarely hesitated to speak her mind was suddenly so silent. If anyone else was aware of how unnaturally quiet she was, Beth didn't notice it. She saw only Ken's reaction, felt only his bewilderment. Regret stole through her. How could she explain to him that she was terrified to make an effort to fit in, terrified of the awful sense of failure that would follow their eventual and inevitable parting?

"Dessert?" Delores asked when everyone had finally pushed back from the table.

Only Claude looked willing. A chorus of *laters* came from everyone else.

"I think a walk is in order," Harriet said.

"There's a game coming on," Claude protested.

"Can I watch with you, Uncle Claude?" Chelsea asked.

"Absolutely. I can tell you how I would be doing it, if I were on the field."

"You're pitiful," Ken teased. "You're resorting to telling your lies to seven-year-old girls now."

Harriet shook her head and Beth and Delores laughed as the bantering disintegrated into a debate about which man had more talent and more know-how.

"I was the quarterback. Everybody knows that's the brains of the team," Ken challenged.

"And I protected your sorry butt," Claude countered. "My apologies, ladies, but that's the gospel truth."

"Just go watch the game," Harriet said. She looked at Beth. "What about you?"

"I'm ready for a walk."

"Delores?"

"I think I'll stay here and clean up."

"Oh, no, you don't. You leave that for us," Harriet protested. "If you don't feel like walking, then sit down someplace and put your feet up."

"I won't do much," Delores promised. "You two have a nice walk. Be careful of the road. There are still some icy patches."

Harriet and Beth bundled up and set off along the stretch of road toward town. The icy air froze their breath. The wind cut through the layers of clothes they'd put on before walking outside. For the next few minutes, after the heavy meal, Beth knew it would feel invigorating. Then they'd be ready to dash back inside to warm up by the fire.

They hadn't gone more than a hundred yards when Harriet said, "So, tell me. Are you in love with Ken?"

Beth lifted startled eyes to meet her gaze and felt a rush of blood in her cheeks. Hopefully Harriet would attribute that to the cold. She managed a weak laugh, then commented, "Direct, aren't you?"

"It's the best way I know to get answers. Ken's like family to Claude and me. We've been worried about him since he and Pam split. She was a real piece of work, nothing at all like Delores. I swear that woman must wonder sometimes if Pam wasn't a changeling. Anyway, we've been afraid the whole experience would sour Ken on marriage. Then out of the blue he goes and decides to settle down all the way up in Vermont. I figure you must have had something to do with that."

Beth shook her head. "I don't think so. He seemed pretty set on settling here when he called me about looking for a house," Beth said, avoiding the real issue Harriet had raised. "He hasn't said much about the past."

"And you haven't asked?" Harriet said incredulously. "Isn't that supposed to be the first question a woman asks a divorced man—how bad was it? The answer tells you a lot about what to expect."

"I suppose I didn't ask because the answer didn't matter," Beth said. "I'm not looking for a serious relationship."

"I didn't ask if you were looking," Harriet reminded her. "Seems to me like one found you." She glanced over. "You getting along okay with Chelsea?"

Beth shrugged, wishing she could confide in this woman who was sensitive enough to guess the potential for conflict between her and Ken's daughter. Still, she was determined to keep her own counsel about this. It wouldn't be fair to discuss her relationship with Ken with his friends.

When Beth didn't answer right away, Harriet added, "Chelsea can be difficult."

"I suppose. We don't spend a lot of time together."

Harriet stopped in her tracks. "I must be getting my signals all mixed up here. I could have sworn that the sparks flying between you and Ken were of an intimate nature. Have I been married so long I've lost my knack?"

Beth blushed.

"Aha. So I'm not going nuts. Is there some reason you're fighting the inevitable? Or need I ask? It is Chelsea, isn't it? She's being a brat. Claude said so, too."

"So far the damage is only minor," Beth admitted, trying to minimize the problem.

"Give her time."

"There are some things time can't fix," Beth said bleakly.

Harriet studied her intently. "You've been through this before, haven't you?" she guessed.

Beth wasn't nearly as stunned by Harriet's intuitiveness as she could have been. "How did you know?"

"You display all the signs of the walking wounded. Have you discussed this with Ken?"

"There's nothing to discuss. It's my problem. I'm just not cut out to be a mother."

"Bull—" the other woman began and cut herself off with a wince. "Sorry. I'm picking up Claude's bad habits."

Beth chuckled at her chagrin. "But sometimes those words are just so much more satisfying and to the point, aren't they?"

"You've got that right, girl." Her expression turned serious again. "Look, I'm a school counselor. Prying is my business and I don't seem to be able to turn it off at the end of the day. So you can ignore me if you want to. You can even tell me to hush up, but not before I tell you that you owe it to yourself and to Ken to be honest with him. Nobody comes into this world a mother. It's something we learn to do by trial and error. Whatever happened in the past probably taught you a few things. Chances are you weren't to blame for most of the problems, anyway. I could cite all sorts of comforting statistics to prove you're not alone. Second marriages are very difficult when there are stepchildren involved. Spread the guilt around a little, why don't you, instead of taking it all on yourself."

"But I was the adult," she said, echoing Peter's oft-spoken refrain.

"That's right," Harriet agreed. "You were the *adult*. Not a saint."

Beth was grateful for her directness and her common sense. "Thanks for the advice."

"You going to take any of it?"

Beth sighed. "I just don't know if I can."

Harriet leveled a gaze at her. "Ken Hutchinson's worth it, girl. He's a decent, caring guy, and despite all the garbage that's been written about him, pro and con, he's come out of football with the same solid values he took into the game. Don't go messing up a chance to have a life with him for all the wrong reasons.''

Ken had no idea what had happened when Beth and Harriet had gone for that walk, but when they returned Beth seemed more at peace. She didn't even flinch when he brought her a piece of pumpkin pie, then lingered on the arm of the chair next to her.

"I'm glad you're here." He leaned down to whisper in her ear.

A tentative smile curved her lips. "Me, too."

In fact, the den, which had been converted into a makeshift TV room for the occasion, seemed to be filled with warmth and goodwill. It was the happiest holiday he could recall for some time. Pam had always insisted on throwing these perfectly orchestrated bashes, which were incredibly successful but far from homey or intimate.

Just as Ken was thinking how much it meant to be surrounded by family and good friends, rather than an entourage of people he barely knew, Claude lumbered to his feet.

"Come on, Harriet. We've got us a plane to catch."

Chelsea immediately protested.

"Sorry, Half-pint, I've got to get ready to go pound on some bad guys on Sunday. I need my beauty rest."

"But you're already beautiful, Uncle Claude," Chelsea proclaimed, tightening her arms around his neck. "Don't go. You're my only friend in the whole wide world."

Ken winced at the plaintive note in his daughter's voice. He and Claude exchanged a look, then his friend held Chelsea up in the air. "Now, you listen to me, young lady. I am not the only friend you have. You've already got a brand-new friend right here in Vermont."

"Who?" Chelsea said doubtfully.

"Beth."

"She's Daddy's friend, not mine."

Ken watched Beth's expression when the blunt assessment popped out of Chelsea's mouth. Some of the color drained out of her face.

"Well, that won't always be the case," Ken said hurriedly. "Now that you're all moved in we'll be doing lots of things together."

"There," Claude said. "I told you so. And pretty soon you'll be going to school here and the next time I come to town I won't be able to take a step for fear of squishing some little munchkin under my big, old feet."

Chelsea laughed at that. "You've never squished me."

"That's because you're so noisy, I always know where you are," he informed her. "You're just like a kitty with a bell around its neck." He planted a smacking kiss on Chelsea's forehead and turned her over to her father, then wrapped his beefy hand around his wife's elbow. "Come on, little mother."

Harriet paused on the front steps and looked straight at Beth. "Don't forget what I said."

"I won't."

When the couple was finally out of sight, Ken looked at Beth. "What was that all about?"

"Girl talk."

He grinned. "Must have been about me."

"Don't look now, but your ego is showing," Delores said.

"What's an ego?" Chelsea demanded.

"Something your daddy has way too much of," Delores said. "Come on, Chelsea. You can help me put the dishes in the dishwasher."

"But I wanted to play a game with Daddy."

"After we get the dishes going," Delores said firmly. Chelsea opened her mouth to offer another protest, but her grandmother already had her firmly by the hand and was leading her away.

Ken captured Beth's hand in his own. "Alone at last."

"I really should help with the dishes," Beth said hurriedly.

"Three sets of hands will only get in the way. Believe me, Delores considers the kitchen her domain and it's good for Chelsea to have chores. Now, come into the den with me and relax. We haven't had a minute to ourselves all day."

"Was there something you wanted to talk to me about?"

He grinned at her worried frown. "Talking was not what I had in mind. Today's Thanksgiving. You're one of the things I'm most thankful for. I thought I should demonstrate how much."

A sigh seemed to ease through her, but her expression turned sad.

"What's wrong?"

"Nothing."

"I don't believe that," he said, sitting in a chair and pulling her into his lap before she could protest. "You've had that expression on your face half a dozen times today. Tell me what it's all about."

"It's just that you're so sweet."

"Sweet, huh? Some guys would consider that an insult."

"Oh, I think you're strong enough to take it," she said, allowing herself the first hint of a smile he'd seen all afternoon.

Ken frowned. "I wish you'd talk to me."

"I talk to you all the time."

He gestured around the room with its remaining piles of wallpaper rolls, paint cans and papers. "About this. Not about anything important."

"This is important."

"*We're* important," he corrected. "All of this is just window dressing."

"You won't feel that way when the wiring goes on the fritz or the plumbing leaks."

"Yes, I will," he insisted. "Wiring and plumbing can be fixed. I'm more worried about us."

"Meaning?"

"I want to get back what we had this time last week. We can't do that as long as you're not being honest with me about what went wrong."

He watched with a sense of resignation as her expression completely shut down. "Beth?" he prodded.

But instead of responding to his question, she visibly distanced herself emotionally, then followed that by physically removing herself from his arms.

"It's been a lovely day," she said in that tight, polite voice that made him want to scream in frustration.

"It could be a lovely evening, as well."

She shook her head. "I really should go. I—I promised Gillie I'd stop by."

Ken knew in his gut that she was lying again. He could read it in her eyes, because she was so damn bad at it. If she actually stopped off to see anyone between his place and home, he would be stunned.

"Are you coming by to work tomorrow?"

She shook her head. "Most of the guys are taking it as a holiday. I thought I would, too."

"Then let's do something together. Chelsea will be starting school on Monday. The next few days will be our only chance to get out and do things just for fun."

He wouldn't have thought it possible, but her expression grew even more distant. "It's important for the two of you to spend this time together," she said stiffly. "She needs you right now."

Ken's temper finally kicked in. "I can't tell if you're truly trying to be unselfish here or if you just don't want to spend time with us. Whichever it is, it's beginning to grate on my nerves."

Her lower lip trembled. "I'm sorry."

He threw up his hands in a gesture of resignation. "Yeah, so am I."

She cast one last look at him, then trudged off through the rapidly deepening snow toward her car.

She looked so forlorn he almost went after her, but then he reminded himself that she had made a clear choice. He'd be damned if he'd force himself on a woman who so plainly no longer wanted any part of him.

But that didn't keep him from standing in the doorway and watching until the red glow of the tail-lights on her car finally faded from view.

Chapter Thirteen

The day after Thanksgiving Ken was still trying to figure out what to make of Beth's abrupt departure when Chet Mathias called.

"Sorry I haven't gotten to you before this, but I've been out of the country," the sporting goods manufacturer explained. "Took my wife on a fortieth anniversary trip all over Europe. I hope to hell I can work until I'm eighty. That's how long it'll take to pay for all the shopping she did. Give that woman foreign currency and she thinks it's play money."

"But you had a good time, didn't you?" Ken retorted.

"The best," he admitted.

"I can hear it in your voice."

"I have to admit I feel better than I have in years. But that's enough about me. You settling in okay? I hear Beth's been helping you."

"She's been a godsend, Chet. I can't thank you enough for recommending her," Ken replied truthfully.

"I thought maybe the two of you..." He allowed the suggestion to trail off, then waited expectantly.

Ken hesitated, then admitted, "We have been out a couple of times. She was here with us for Thanksgiving yesterday."

"Perfect. I knew first time I met you that the two of you would get along. Tried my darnedest to figure out a way to make it happen, but matchmaking schemes aren't exactly my bailiwick and my wife Corinne flatly refused to meddle. Then when you called last month, well, it just seemed like everything was falling into place."

"How much do you know about Beth?" Ken asked.

"Not much about the time before she came here. She doesn't say too much about her past. I've always been a believer in looking at what a person's made of now and not worrying too much about how they got that way." He laughed. "Just look at me. Forty years ago, I was nobody's idea of a good bet. Corinne was the only woman brave enough to take a chance on me. As for Beth, I could see right off that the lady was all class. Maybe a little on the quiet side, but definitely all class."

Ken wasn't about to argue with that assessment, but he needed more. "So you don't know anything about her marriage," he said.

"Marriage?" Chet sounded genuinely astounded. "Hell, I didn't even know she'd been married. Well, I'll be darned. Is that a problem for you?"

"Of course not. I just get the feeling it is for her, but she won't talk about it."

"Well, I'll be darned," Chet said, still sounding stunned. "You know that friend of hers, Gillie Townsend?"

"Beth has spoken of her. We haven't met."

"Then I'd say a meeting is past due. She's usually down at Lou's after she drops her kids off at school. Fact is, I think one of her kids is about the same age as your daughter, so you'll surely be getting to know her. My guess is that she knows Beth as well as anyone around these parts."

"I'll keep that in mind," Ken said, trying to imagine himself going up to a total stranger and pumping her for information about a woman with whom he'd already been intimate. He doubted he could pull it off.

If the two women were as close as Chet had surmised, Gillie might know about his relationship with Beth and tell him to ask Beth directly, if there was something he wanted to know. If she didn't know about him, he would feel thoroughly underhanded. More important, Beth would probably string him up if she ever found out about it. And there wasn't a doubt in his mind that she would discover he'd been asking questions. Her best friend wouldn't keep that information a secret.

"Listen, Ken," Chet said, breaking into his thoughts. "Corinne's been busting my chops ever since I got on the phone to invite you to dinner tomorrow night. You free?"

"I'd love to come."

"You want to ask Beth?"

"To tell you the truth, Chet, I'm not at all sure she'd agree to come with me."

"Mind if we ask her, then?"

Ken couldn't help chuckling at how pitiful he'd become, allowing someone else to arrange his dates for him. It was a darn good thing Claude didn't know about this. Ken would never hear the end of it.

"Ask her," he said. "Maybe I'll call her later and offer to give her a lift. Surely she wouldn't refuse a neighborly gesture like that."

"Surely," Chet agreed heartily. "Seven o'clock?"

"Sounds good. Tell Corinne I'm looking forward to seeing all the things she brought back from the trip."

"Lordy, son, don't say that. We'll never get dinner on the table. Now if you want to take a look at my slides—"

"On second thought..."

"Traitor," he accused, laughing. "See you tomorrow, son. We'll be looking forward to it."

Ken knew Chet would waste no time tracking Beth down. Nor did he doubt for a minute that the older man could talk her into coming to a dinner party. It remained to be seen, though, whether his own powers of persuasion would be equally successful. He waited until that evening to call.

"Beth, it's Ken."

"Oh, hello," she said, sounding cautious. "Is something wrong?"

He decided to ignore her assumption that he wouldn't call unless there was a problem. He also decided not to give her a chance to refuse his offer to pick her up for the dinner party. Didn't women tend to respond to confidence in a man? Or had that changed in the years since he'd been out of the dating scene?

"I just wanted to let you know I'd be by about six-thirty tomorrow to pick you up," he said matter-of-factly.

"Six-thirty? Tomorrow?"

"That's right. You are going to Chet's, aren't you?"

"Well, yes, but—"

"I told him I'd pick you up."

"You...told...him," she began, enunciating every word very carefully.

Ken grinned. She was royally ticked, all right. Hallelujah! He'd rather have her screaming at him than sinking into that quiet sadness he'd witnessed all too often. "Sure. I don't mind. You're not a bit out of my way."

"You don't mind," she said, her voice climbing.

"Is there a problem?" he inquired, injecting a note of innocence into his voice.

"Yes, there's a problem. First, I had no idea you'd even been invited. Second, I certainly had no idea you would dare to assume you would be my date. Third..."

She seemed at a loss to come up with anything else. Ken bit back a chuckle. "Third?" he prompted.

"Third, you are making me crazy."

He could no longer hold back the laughter.

"What's so damn funny?" she snapped irritably.

"You. You're fighting the inevitable, sweetheart."

"There's nothing inevitable about any of this and I am not your sweetheart. I am not your anything!"

"I suppose that's a matter of perspective," he conceded thoughtfully. "It's how I think of you, but perhaps you haven't quite gotten to that stage yet."

Beth heaved a sigh. "Why are you doing this?"

"Doing what?"

"Chasing after something that just can't be. Anyway, I thought you were furious with me."

"I was. It didn't last. The truth is, Ms. Callahan, I find you perplexing, frustrating, irritating and incredibly attractive."

"Most of those weren't even good traits," she noted pointedly.

"I know. Just shows you how perverse I can be. So, do we have a date or not?"

"We absolutely, positively do *not* have a date," she said very distinctly.

"Oh," he said, defeated.

"But you may pick me up at six-thirty."

He sucked in a deep breath and tried not to shout for joy. "See you then," he said, and hurriedly hung up before he lost even a sliver of the tiny bit of ground he'd gained.

This dinner party was a mistake, Beth thought as she pulled on a simple red wool dress, added diamond stud earrings and slipped into a pair of heels.

Actually, the dinner wasn't the problem. She adored Chet and Corinne. It was the drive to and from that promised to be exasperating and dangerous.

She still didn't understand why Ken was so persistent in the face of her obvious reluctance to get more deeply involved with him. Perhaps it had something to do with the fact that she'd already slept with him, she thought wryly. Maybe he figured that suggested they were already pretty seriously involved. Maybe he figured that had meant something to her.

And maybe he was right, she conceded wearily. It had meant something. But that didn't mean she couldn't forget about it, if she tried hard enough. She just had to keep her distance, which was absolutely not possible in a cozy car on a starlit night unless she rode in the back seat. She doubted he'd go for that, not without an explanation. And telling him she was scared to death to be near him would create more problems than it would solve.

She paced through the house tidying up things that didn't need to be tidied. When the doorbell finally rang, promptly at six-thirty, she jumped as if it had been a gunshot. After one last glance in the hallway mirror, she opened the door. She took one look at Ken and her jaw went slack.

Oh, dear Heaven. It was the first time she had ever seen him all dressed up in a suit and tie. Obviously he knew how Corinne felt about dressing up for dinner. He was wearing a wool overcoat that looked as if it had cost twice the commission she was likely to make on the restoration of his house. Though it was obvious he'd carefully blown his hair dry in a neat style, it was already sexily tousled by the wind.

"You look . . ." she began.

"You look . . ." he said at the same time.

"Fantastic," they said in a murmured chorus.

He grinned. "I guess it's unanimous. We're going to knock 'em dead."

Beth flushed with pleasure and tried valiantly to ignore the way the gleam in his eyes made her feel. It was amazing that with one glance he could boost her self-confidence as a woman to new heights. If only it were as easy to restore her self-esteem as a mother.

The rest of the evening passed in a blur. Chet was a lavish, thoughtful host, as always. Corinne's dinner was superb. But it was Ken's quiet attentiveness that kept Beth glowing with an undeniable inner heat and a sense of expectation. Alone, with just the two of them, she dared to think that anything was possible. At least for this one night.

Being with Ken, feeling his body harden in response to her touch, breathing in the clean, masculine scent of him, giving herself to him until they were both crying out with the sheer exhilaration of their passion . . .

Those were the things she wanted, she finally admitted to herself. Those were the things she imagined on the quiet drive home. The images were so vivid that her pulse raced and her blood sizzled in anticipation.

In the soft glow of an old-fashioned streetlamp, Ken cut the engine and turned to her. His gaze locked with hers until she was trembling, wishing with every fiber that he would close the distance between them. He reached across and gently trailed a finger across her lips and left them quivering. The sensation ricocheted all the way through her.

"I want you," he said softly.

Beth swallowed hard. "I want you," she confessed.

"Then why is this so damn complicated?"

"It's not," she protested, even though she knew far more than he exactly how complicated it was. An admission, though, she knew with absolute certainty, would cost her dearly. She would lose not just the future, but tonight. This breathless moment.

"When I hold you or touch you, it's not," he agreed. "But all the other times . . ." His gaze studied her sorrowfully. "All the other times, you keep such distance between us."

"I didn't put it there."

"Then who did?"

Your daughter, she wanted to scream. *Your little girl.*

But she kept silent, because to say it would invite questions for which she had no answers.

Ken's eyes filled with something that might have been dismay. "There it is again," he said wearily. "The sadness. I can't know what to do about it, if you won't tell me what's causing it."

Tears of quiet despair pooled in her eyes, then spilled down her cheeks. "You couldn't fix it, if you knew," she said bleakly, opening the car door and stepping into the frigid night air that instantly froze the tears on her cheeks. She simply couldn't bear to tell him what a failure she had been as a mother. Right now he might be confused about why she had withdrawn from him, but at least he saw her as a complete woman. She had his respect. If he knew everything, nothing would change...except the way he looked at her. She wasn't sure she could bear that.

Even though she knew that parting now was best, all the way to the house she prayed he would follow. She listened for the car door, but heard nothing until, at last, the engine turned over and he slowly pulled away, the tires crunching on the ice.

Chelsea stood in the middle of her bedroom on Monday morning and pitched a tantrum that had Delores near tears and Ken ready to pack everything and head back to Washington.

"I won't go! I won't," she screamed, taking off school clothes as fast as Delores could dress her in them.

Ken's patience finally snapped, but somehow by the grace of God he managed to remain calm. "Delores, I'll handle this," he said finally. He figured this was one crisis he couldn't hand off to anyone else.

She regarded him worriedly. "Ken, maybe it would be better if—"

"No, it's okay. You go downstairs and put breakfast on the table. I want Chelsea to have a nice hot meal before she goes off to her first day of school here."

Delores nodded and left. Chelsea watched him warily, tears pooling in her eyes and streaking down her flushed cheeks.

"I won't go," she whispered, chin wobbling.

"Okay, let's talk about this." He held out his arms, but his daughter stood stiffly right where she was. Obviously she'd gotten her stubborn streak from him. "Why don't you want to go to school?"

"Because..."

"Not good enough. Because why?"

Huge eyes that could break a father's heart stared back at him. "Because I don't know...anybody... here." The words were punctuated by renewed sobs.

Ken sighed. "Shortstuff, the only way you'll make new friends here is by going to school. Remember when you went to school for the very first time? You didn't know anybody then either. First thing you knew you had lots of friends."

"That was different."

"Different how?"

Tiny shoulders heaved. "Mmm...Mmm...Mommy went with me."

His own tears clogging his throat, Ken reached for Chelsea and this time she didn't resist. She clung to him with all of her seven-year-old strength. "Sweetie, I'm going to go with you today. And I won't leave you there alone until you tell me it's okay. I promise."

She sniffed and regarded him distrustfully. "Really?"

"Absolutely."

"And if I want to come back home?"

He shook his head at that. "Sorry. That's not an option. So, how about it? Do we have a deal?"

"You won't go until I say so?" she said one more time.

"No. I promise."

She considered that thoughtfully, then finally nodded. "I guess that would be okay."

Two hours later, just as Ken had anticipated, Chelsea was caught up in the second grade class's activities and paying absolutely no attention to him. When it was time for a juice break and recess, she ran over and said with an air of grown-up nonchalance. "You can go now."

He grinned at her. "Having fun?"

"It's not like my old school, but it's okay, I guess."

He gave her a quick hug. "I'm glad. I'll see you this afternoon."

Not until he was walking back to his car did he finally allow himself a moment to savor a major parenting victory. If only he could solve the dilemma he was facing with Beth as easily.

The next week was hell. Just as Beth came to accept that Ken would rarely stay in the house while she was there, Beth slowly grew used to finding Chelsea peering at her from the doorway to Ken's office the minute she came in the door from school. As painful as it was, she came to expect the child to shadow her as she put the finishing touches on each room. Chelsea rarely said a word and neither did Beth. But Chelsea's apparent loneliness since her grandmother had returned to Washington spoke volumes. If she was making new friends at school, there was no sign of them at home. Ken had hired a housekeeper, but Chelsea seemed to distrust her even more than she did Beth.

Beth's heart ached every time she looked into Chelsea's sad, expectant eyes, but she steeled herself against the reaction. She would not lower her defenses. She would not love this child, who wielded such power over her father's life. She didn't dare.

The tantrums helped. They were frequent enough and disturbing enough to strengthen Beth's resolve. Those tantrums were just more demonstrative expressions of the same hateful behavior she'd experienced with Josh and Stephanie. She was sure if Chelsea could have run away from home, she would have. If she had been old enough to think of being sneakily spiteful, Beth was sure she would have done that, too.

Instead Chelsea's sabotage was less sophisticated and more open. She stole into the room whenever she sensed that Beth and Ken were sharing an all-too-rare quiet moment that excluded her. Not content that her presence alone was interruption enough, she usually managed to break something or spill something or demand attention in some other way that required an immediate response or punishment. Beth recognized that Ken was at his wit's end, but so was she. She'd bitten her tongue so often this past week, she was surprised the tip was still attached. It was ironic, too. Chelsea was trying to spoil a relationship that was already dead.

"Can I help?" Chelsea asked in a small voice after watching Beth put the hooks into the drapes for the living room.

"Sure," Beth said, reluctant to include her, but just as uneasy with saying no. She couldn't bring herself to be mean to this child, no matter the cost to herself.

Every time she looked into Chelsea's face, she saw the man she loved.

To her dismay, Chelsea settled right beside her, her little body snuggled close as she tried to mimic Beth's actions. Beth breathed in the little girl scent of her, the mix of shampoo and lotion and freshly ironed clothes. Her fingers suddenly became all thumbs as she fought to resist the urge to hug the child who so desperately needed to be reassured.

"Is this right?" Chelsea asked, her gray eyes fastened on Beth's face as her fingers fumbled with the hook.

"Exactly right," she answered.

"I got an *A* in school today," Chelsea confided. "My teacher said I'm the very best speller she's ever seen."

"That's wonderful! Your father will be really proud."

"Maybe he'll take me for pizza tonight."

"Maybe," Beth agreed.

"You could come, too," she said shyly. "If you want."

Beth's heart slammed against her ribs at the first tiny gesture of friendship Chelsea had ever offered. "We'll see," she said, her voice choked.

"Don't you like pizza?" Chelsea asked, studying her intently.

"It's not that."

Before she could explain, though, Chelsea's eyes filled with tears as she jumped up. "It's me, isn't it? You just don't want to be with me. You're just like my mommy. She couldn't wait to leave me."

She moved so fast, Beth couldn't catch her. Her heart aching, she searched the house room by room, trying not to alarm the housekeeper in the process. Finally, downstairs again, she noticed that the back door was ajar.

At that point, sheer panic and instinct took over. Running outside, she followed the tiny footprints through the snow until she came to the pond. Chelsea was standing at the edge, her expression forlorn, tears still tracking down her cheeks. Without a coat, she was shivering violently.

Beth took her own jacket and wrapped it around her, then knelt down in front of her. "I'm sorry," she said softly. "I never, ever meant to make you think I didn't like you."

"But you don't, do you? You never want to be with me."

"Darling, it's far more complicated than that. And it doesn't have anything to do with you. It has to do with something that happened a long time ago."

Chelsea watched her with solemn eyes. "With another little girl?"

Beth nodded. "And a boy."

"Did you go away and leave them?"

The painful question cut right through her. "I did, but not because I didn't love them."

"Why did you go away, then?"

"Because they didn't love me," she finally admitted with a sigh. Before she could reveal any more to a child far too young to understand the details of what had happened, she added briskly, "Now, quick, let's get you back inside before you catch cold."

Chelsea tucked a hand in Beth's as they walked back to the house. "Beth?"

"What is it, sweetheart?"

"I really miss my mommy."

Tears stung Beth's eyes. "I know you do, but I'm sure you'll get to see her really, really soon. In the meantime, I know she misses you just as much as you miss her."

"I don't think so," Chelsea said with a resigned sigh. "She almost never, ever calls me." She turned a hopeful look on Beth. "Do you think maybe she's lost the phone number?"

"I'll bet that's it," Beth said. "Maybe your daddy can call her tonight and remind her. Would you like me to ask him to do that?"

"Would you?"

"I promise," she said.

Back inside, she made hot chocolate for the two of them and put some of the cookies Delores had baked on a plate. By then Chelsea's color was better and she had stopped shivering, but a familiar silence had fallen between the two of them. This time, though, Beth felt certain there was less tension in it.

That was the way they were when Ken came in.

"Hi, Daddy," Chelsea said as nonchalantly as if this was the scene he found every day when he came in. "Beth made hot chocolate. Want some?"

His gaze pinned on Beth's face, he nodded. "Hot chocolate sounds terrific. It's cold outside."

"I know. I ran out without my coat, but Beth came after me and she gave me hers."

Beth winced at the innocent revelation. "It's a long story."

"I'll bet." He looked at Chelsea. "Why don't you take your snack up to your room and watch TV for a little while before dinner."

When Chelsea had gone, he sat down across from Beth, his hands clenched, his expression grim.

"I think we'd better talk about it," he said.

"She was upset. She ran out without her coat. I found her right afterward. She couldn't have been out there more than five minutes."

"I don't care about that. Obviously, she's fine." His gaze captured hers and held. "I hate the distance between us. I hate the distance between you and Chelsea. Do you realize that this is the first time I have ever seen the two of you together?"

"We're here in the house almost every afternoon."

"But you're not talking. She tiptoes around you and you ignore her."

"I wasn't aware that I'd been hired as a babysitter," she said, her voice tight.

Ken sighed. "That's not the point and you know it. There is something about being around Chelsea that you find upsetting. Please tell me what it is." His gaze was unrelenting. "Please."

His voice was quiet, downright gentle in fact, but there was no mistaking his determination. Beth tried to evade that gaze, but he touched her chin and forced her to face him.

"What is this all about, Beth? Whatever it is, it can't be so terrible that you can't share it with me."

Maybe it was because her nerves were ragged from the days of tension. Maybe it was because she wanted so desperately for everything to be all right. Maybe it was because she genuinely believed what he was saying, that he would understand.

And so, she told him. About her marriage to Peter. About his two handsome children. And about her terrible failure to make it all work.

"They didn't just dislike me," she said, her eyes dry. She was sure there were no tears left to shed over the tragedy of it. "They hated me. They wanted their mother, not a poor substitute. No matter what I did, it was never good enough. I failed Peter and I failed them."

She faced him and injected a note of pure bravado into her voice. "So, as you can see, obviously I'm not anyone's idea of the perfect mother." She said it with a cavalier shrug, but Ken didn't seem to be buying her act.

"Oh, baby," he whispered, and pulled her close as a fresh batch of tears spilled down her cheeks and soaked his shirt. "Don't you see, that's nonsense. You're warm and generous and caring. Any child would be lucky to have you for a mother. Just look at what happened here this afternoon."

She sniffed. "Right. I upset Chelsea so badly she went tearing outside, where she could have caught pneumonia."

"She didn't look traumatized when I came home. How do you suppose that happened?"

"Hot chocolate can smooth over a lot."

"If that were all it took, wouldn't you have used that on your stepchildren?" he said dryly.

"I suppose so."

"Look, I'm sure Chelsea's behavior since her arrival has done absolutely nothing to reassure you, but she's scared, too. She's afraid to reach out to someone who'll turn around and abandon her the way her mother did. I've probably been more tolerant than I should have been, but I assure you it won't be that way forever. I'm feeling my way as a single parent. It would make things a lot easier if I had you by my side, telling me if I'm making the right choices."

"I'm the last person to be giving anyone advice about parenting."

"It's not advice I want, so much as moral support."

"But Chelsea and I..." She held her hands up in a helpless gesture.

"I don't expect you and Chelsea to get along perfectly. Haven't you noticed that there are plenty of times when she and I don't get along worth a damn?"

"But you're her father."

"That doesn't come with guarantees or instructions." He tilted her chin up. "Try. Please. I know it's a risk. I know how fragile your self-confidence must be. But wouldn't the payoff be worth it?"

"Payoff," she repeated slowly.

"We might turn out to be a real family. That's what I want," he insisted. "More than anything."

A family, Beth repeated to herself. If she searched her heart, wasn't that what she really desperately wanted, as well?

Chapter Fourteen

Delores had nailed it, Ken thought later that night. Once again his ex-mother-in-law had seen a situation with far clearer vision than his own. She had picked up on Beth's uneasiness around Chelsea immediately and labeled it anxiety rather than distaste. He'd been skeptical that a woman as strong as Beth could be controlled by fear of anything, especially a little girl. If only he'd listened to Delores, he might have solved this problem much sooner.

Still, now that he recognized that Beth's behavior was the result of something from her past, not dislike of Chelsea or children in general, he could do something about it. He could begin to reassure her that loving him and Chelsea would not be a repeat of the past.

Suddenly he felt free to allow his own growing feelings for her to flourish again, after days of trying to talk them out of existence. He had hated the sense of powerlessness her behavior had instilled in him. Now, at last, he was back in control.

Unfortunately, he doubted that Beth was going to be easily persuaded that her fears were groundless. Others had done that, had convinced her to ignore her instincts, and look what had happened to her first marriage. Now she would be a much tougher sell, much slower to believe that time could correct today's problems between Chelsea and any woman who wasn't her mother.

At the same time, he recognized that Chelsea could hardly be won over by a woman who wouldn't dare any overture that might be rebuffed. Given the nature of their fears, they might very well have faced a stalemate.

Fortunately, though, Ken had had a lot of experience at faking out defensive backs on some of the best teams in the NFL. Surely he could pull off a few sneaky maneuvers to allow one terrified lady and one pint-size hellion to discover what he already knew—they desperately needed each other.

And he needed them both, more and more with each passing day. The two of them had made his transition from star quarterback to private citizen an easy one. He had found all sorts of quiet satisfaction in raising his daughter, even when she was at her worst. He had found another sort of contentment entirely with Beth. Those discoveries made him more determined than ever to work things out. He was falling in love with her and he knew that what they had was based on a solid foundation, the kind of foundation that could last a lifetime.

The truth of it was, if he hadn't believed in his own future with Beth with all his heart, he wouldn't have dared to set her and his daughter up for the eventual pain of another separation. His love, which had taken no one more by surprise than him, was growing stronger—strong enough to battle whatever lay ahead.

Over the next couple of weeks, Ken's campaign strategy was worthy of Super Bowl play. He had discovered on that fateful afternoon when Beth had finally revealed her painful past to him that she and Chelsea were far more likely to reach out to each other, if they weren't under his watchful eye.

He changed the housekeeper's hours, giving her most afternoons off. He suddenly found a dozen excuses to go into town every day about three o'clock, leaving Beth to welcome Chelsea home from school. After the first day or two, Beth no longer protested. The wariness began to fade.

Two or three times a week he suggested dinner, a video, a shopping excursion. He made the suggestions to Chelsea, then casually extended the invitation to Beth, as well. She could hardly refuse with Chelsea's solemn gray eyes pinned on her. Ken sensed that with every passing day, Beth was less inclined to turn them down, that in fact she was beginning to look forward to sharing these times with them.

The weekdays, as a result of his careful timing and nonthreatening suggestions, were easy. It was weekend outings that required incredibly deft planning, especially as the holiday season approached and Christmas festivities began in earnest in Berry Ridge. Beth, it seemed, was involved in everything, quite possibly, he guessed, to keep the loneliness at bay.

At any rate, if he wanted to take the two of them out to a movie in a neighboring town, he had to be clever and quick about it. He discovered if he found an antique store in between and assured Beth that he really needed her input on some piece of furniture he'd spotted for the house, she was always more ready to accept. As a result, he spent hours during the week hunting down such stores and furniture and found, to his amazement, that it was fun. There was no way Beth could mistake his enthusiasm for guile.

Then, once they'd settled on whether to buy the chair or table or cabinet, it was easy enough to suggest that they go on to lunch and then a movie or perhaps Christmas shopping or a visit to Santa.

Pretty soon Beth was suggesting outings that Chelsea might enjoy—a visit to a woman who made quilts, an excursion to see apple cider pressed, a drive into Woodstock where there were four churchbells made by Paul Revere, a Christmas bazaar, an old-fashioned community potpie dinner in a neighboring town, a night of caroling.

He saw Beth slowly healing before his very eyes. She seemed to have an endless supply of patience for Chelsea's inquisitiveness. She no longer looked stung by an innocently sharp remark or a sullen expression. And he found in her courage yet another reason for his growing feelings for her.

As Beth's anxiety lessened, the bond between her and his daughter grew stronger each day. Giving them the space to find their own way, he rejoiced when Chelsea automatically slipped her mittened hand into Beth's. He took tremendous satisfaction when Beth instinctively knelt down and tucked Chelsea's scarf around her neck and buttoned her coat more tightly against the ever-more frigid air. Beth was, as he had always guessed, a nurturing woman, and now that side of her had a chance to flourish, surrounding his daughter in much-needed feminine warmth.

As the icy reserve began to thaw between the two females in his life, Ken might have felt left out of their laughter, jealous of their silly banter, envious of the quiet times they shared over hot chocolate and one of Chelsea's favorite books or puzzles.

Instead, he discovered that even when he was excluded, he was a sucker for their tender, warm rapport. He basked in their genuine enjoyment of the time they spent together. And as he closely observed this sexy, radiant, sensitive woman, his own hormones blazed hotter than the wood stove he'd installed in his kitchen.

Unfortunately, it was incredibly difficult to seduce a woman with a seven-year-old chaperon constantly along. He weighed the importance of the bond between Chelsea and Beth against his own needs and told himself he'd just have to keep sight of his goal, and take a lot of very cold showers.

He also had a plan that, with any luck, would bring an end to this self-enforced abstinence. He stood in the doorway of his den one night and watched Beth as she went over the last of the invoices. The house was essentially finished, its wallpaper brand-new from top to bottom, the wood floors polished to a gleam, the molding repaired and painted, the drapes hung. He almost regretted that the happy chaos was over. He wondered if she felt the same way or if her sense of pride in her accomplishment made up for any regrets that she was through with her renovations of her beloved Grady place.

Ken smiled. She still called it that, correcting herself in midphrase with a rueful grin. To her, it would always be the Grady place, even if he could someday persuade her to call it home.

He looked up and caught her watching him.

"What are you smiling about?" she asked.

"You."

She sat back and regarded him warily. "I see. And what about me has you smiling?"

He shrugged. "I have no idea. I just like looking at you, I suppose." He gestured toward the invoices. "Just about done?"

"Yep. The last of the bills are paid. I told you you'd be settled before Christmas."

"The job's not quite over," he informed her.

"Oh?"

"We have holiday decorating to do and entertaining. I'm at a loss."

She shook her head. "Ken Hutchinson, you've never been at a loss in your life. Who are you trying to kid?"

"You don't believe me?" he said, injecting a wounded note into his voice.

"I don't believe you."

"Okay, take a Christmas tree, for instance. Where do I get one?"

"There's a small lot by town hall or you can go into the woods and cut one down."

"What do you do?"

"I dig one up, then replant it in my yard after the holiday."

"Ecology-minded. I like that. Where do we go?"

"We?"

"Sure. You don't expect me to do this on my own, do you? We'll go on Saturday. Chelsea can come, too. She'll love it." He saw temptation written all over her face and knew that he had won yet another battle. "Eight o'clock?"

"Eight?" she said doubtfully.

"You know perfectly well you're up by dawn. We'll have breakfast first at Lou's," he said decisively. "Pancakes and warm maple syrup."

She laughed. "How do you manage to make food sound so seductive?"

"It's your wild imagination," he retorted. "First thing you know, you're picturing the two of us sharing those pancakes in bed."

"Now that is a thought," she admitted. Her voice was surprisingly and deliberately provocative and sent his pulse racing.

"Saturday," he repeated in a suddenly choked voice, then ducked out of the room before he was tempted to make love to her right there in the middle of his big, solid desk.

* * *

Beth had figured out what Ken was up to the first time he'd managed to lure her into accompanying him and Chelsea on some outing. She had clung to her resistance to his charms and his daughter's increasingly warm reception for days, but slowly she had given up fighting the longing she had to spend time with the two of them.

Each time, though, she swore would be the last. Though the number of successful, stress-free outings had mounted, there was always a nagging worry in the back of her mind that the next one would be a disaster. Chelsea might be accepting her as a friend, but that might be more by default than any real affection. What would happen if she feared that Beth was trying to take her mother's place? Beth was certain she knew the answer to that and it lurked on the fringes of her mind, spoiling any genuine joy she might have taken in the time she shared with Ken's precious daughter.

She found she was dreading the approaching holidays. No other time of year was more meant to be shared by families. Ken's determination to act as if that was what they were was as frightening as it was tempting.

This Christmas tree outing, for instance. It was just one more link in the emotional chain binding her to them. What would happen to her when the chain broke? It would be so much worse than last time, because over the past few weeks she had had a real taste of the promised sweetness of motherhood and the blessing of being loved—by father and child. It was more fulfilling than anything she had ever experienced or imagined.

There was no way to get out of the tree excursion, though. Every one of Ken's invitations was issued almost as a dare. He was asking her to take a risk. On him. On Chelsea. On the three of them. If he was willing to take such a dangerous chance, how could she do any less?

On Saturday morning, she walked to Lou's, wanting the quiet solitude to steel herself against the tender torment of the day ahead. Fresh snow had fallen overnight, blanketing the ground with a fluffy layer of white that caught the sun and glistened like a scattering of diamonds across soft, white velvet. Every shop window twinkled with Christmas lights and tempted with holiday decorations. Soft carols, piped over a loudspeaker system, broke the morning's silence. She stopped for a moment just to listen.

Oh, how she loved this town with its sense of community, its centuries' old traditions, its untainted beauty. Her growing feelings for Ken and for his daughter, only brought it all into sharper focus. This was a good place to raise a family, a good place to love, a good place to fulfill cherished dreams, a good place to grow old. Would all of that happen for her? Or would it slip away?

She looked up then and saw Ken waiting for her in front of Lou's bakery. He was leaning against the side of his car, his long legs crossed at the ankles, his arms folded across his middle as he watched her. Smiling, her heart suddenly light, she picked up her pace.

As she drew closer, she sniffed the air and, even from half a block away, she could smell the scent of fresh-baked cinnamon rolls, sizzling bacon and fresh-brewed coffee. As a lure, it was almost as powerful as the man waiting for her.

"A bit chilly for a leisurely stroll, don't you think?" he teased her.

"It's all in knowing how many layers to put on."

He grinned and reached for the top button of her jacket, drawing her close. "Too bad we're not some-place I can strip them off and count them."

She gave him her sassiest smile. "It is too bad, isn't it?"

He laughed as she swept past him and went inside. She spotted Chelsea seated in a back booth, already telling Lou what she wanted for breakfast. She scowled up at the two of them.

"I didn't think you were ever going to get here," she said, bouncing in her impatience to get the day under way.

Lou chuckled. "You two want coffee?"

"And food," Ken said. "We need lots of energy for the day we have planned."

"I hear you're going to find a Christmas tree."

"Two trees," Beth corrected. "One for me."

"And a really, really big one for me," Chelsea chimed in.

"I can't wait to see them."

"You'll have to come by on Christmas day," Ken said, surprising Beth. "We're going to have an open house from four to six."

Lou accepted readily, then went off to fill their order.

"An open house?" Beth said when she'd gone. "Sounds like a lot of work."

He grinned. "That's why I'll need your help."

"How will it look if you and I throw this party together?"

"As if we're a couple," he said readily. "Which we are."

"Oh?"

"Sure. Everyone in town knows that."

Unfortunately, Beth knew that was true. Gillie had been the first to pronounce them that when Beth had finally seen her elusive friend again. Invitations issued to the two of them had been arriving in her mailbox for the last week. It seemed a little late to start protesting the obvious. Surely she could get through the holidays before sitting down and explaining to Ken one more time why there was no future for them. He'd been lulled into a false sense of complacency by this détente between her and Chelsea. It wouldn't last, though. She knew that with everything in her.

But she did have today and tomorrow and the next ten days or so beyond that, days she could cram with memories. She smiled as she gazed into Chelsea's excited face and listened to her description of the tree they were going to find and where it was going to sit and how it should be decorated.

An hour later as they were trudging through the snow with Chelsea atop her father's shoulders, Beth realized that her resolve wasn't worth spit. Her defenses were toppling more rapidly than a house of cards in a stiff breeze. She wanted what she had found with Ken and Chelsea, wanted it with a desperation that she had fought and fought, all to no apparent avail.

Ken began the caroling as they ventured up and down the rows in an area that had been specifically forested for Christmas trees. Soon they were all singing, their voices wildly off-key, the words made up half the time when none of them could recall the right verses. They went from *Jingle Bells* to *Silent Night*, from *Rudolph, the Red-Nosed Reindeer* to *Joy to the World,* an eclectic mix of holiday songs that captured the season's true spirit. Beth thought she might very well burst from sheer happiness.

After begging to be allowed down in the snow, Chelsea ran up and down the rows, picking first one tree and then another, while Beth and Ken followed at a more leisurely pace. Beth spotted the perfect tree first, a dream Christmas tree with wide, sweeping branches that would hold an array of glittering ornaments and blinking colored lights. It was too big for her house by far, but in Ken's . . .

She stopped in front of it, just as Chelsea ran up, wide-eyed, and halted beside her. When a tiny mittened hand slipped into her own, Beth thought her heart might very well burst from all of the unexpected emotions crowding in.

"It's beautiful," Chelsea said, clearly awestruck.

"The prettiest tree I've ever seen," Beth agreed.

"It'll take up the whole living room," Ken grumbled, one hand resting on Chelsea's shoulder, the other on Beth's. "We'll have to take a foot off the top and take down the door, just to get it into the house."

"Daddy, please," Chelsea said.

Beth just looked at him imploringly. She was as determined as Chelsea and apparently Ken could see it. And he was clearly in a benevolent sort of mood, ready to grant wishes.

"Oh, for goodness' sake, I'll go tell the man this is the one we want," he grumbled, but Beth noticed he was grinning as he walked away.

They put the huge fir tree on top of Ken's wagon, then found Beth's smaller tree and put it in the back. They stopped by her house long enough to leave her tree propped up beside the back door.

"Do you have enough decorations?" she asked them. "I might have extras."

"We have plenty of lights," Ken said. "And I think I put one big box of ornaments in the attic."

"And the angel for the top," Chelsea said. "I saw it after we moved."

"It's a big tree," Beth warned.

"Which is why I bought popcorn and bags of cranberries," Ken informed her. "While I get this monster put up, you and Chelsea can start stringing them."

"I've never done that, Daddy."

"Neither have I," Beth said.

Ken glanced at her, amazement written all over his face. "But it's tradition."

"Whose?" she grumbled. "In California, the decorator did the tree and I guarantee you there were no strings of popcorn or cranberries involved."

There were so many things she'd missed in a household that had seemed to have everything. Some part of her, though, had always known what Christmas should be like, what families were supposed to share. Her parents, while giving her everything material, had offered her nothing of themselves. She knew that was why motherhood had mattered so much to her, why she had so desperately wanted to get it right. And why she had been so devastated when she hadn't.

"Then making these decorations will be a new experience for all of us," Ken said cheerfully. "An old-fashioned, New England Christmas."

Two hours later Beth had jabbed her fingers with a needle more times than she cared to recall. She had bitten back a stream of curses. But she couldn't help getting a warm feeling deep inside whenever she glanced at the frown of concentration on Chelsea's face as she labored over the lengthening strand of deep red cranberries or the pleasure in Ken's eyes as he watched the two of them.

They stopped at midafternoon for soup and sandwiches, then got back to work. At five they realized the box of elegant, expensive decorations they'd brought from Washington, even with the incongruous addition of several strands of cranberry and popcorn, was woefully inadequate.

"There's still time to get to town before the stores close," Ken said. "Let's go. We can have dinner afterward at the inn, then finish up here."

At the craft store, Chelsea found charming handmade wooden ornaments that were a startling contrast to the fragile glass balls they had brought to

Vermont with them. In her delight over each one, it was obvious she didn't care that the tree would be a mismatched hodgepodge. Nor did Ken seem to care that he was spending a fortune on his daughter's whimsical choices.

"You haven't chosen any," he said to Beth after Chelsea had been at it for a while.

"It's your tree, yours and Chelsea's. You should have what you want."

He frowned at the deliberate distancing. "It's *our* tree," he insisted.

Beth shrugged. It wasn't worth arguing over and spoiling an otherwise perfect day.

He grabbed her hand and led her to the display of ornaments. "Pick something out," he insisted, his jaw set.

"Ken," she began, but the protest died on her lips as she read his expression. She had seen one just as stubborn on Chelsea's face often enough. "Okay," she finally agreed.

She fingered the wooden, hand-painted drummer boys, the miniature white doves, the colorful musical instruments, all carved by local craftsmen. She admired them all.

But it was a handblown glass angel that she loved. The glass was as fragile as a snowflake and just as cool to the touch. Pale traces of color had been blown into the piece, making it shimmer like a rainbow. It was meant for the top of the tree and she knew that Ken and Chelsea already had their angel, so she put it back, trying to hide her longing to own the lovely keepsake ornament.

She reached for a charming wooden nutcracker instead. "This one."

Ken shook his head. "I don't think so."

"You told me to choose."

"I know. And you did," he said, picking up the angel and handing it to the clerk. "We'll take this one, too." His gaze caught Beth's and held. "It will always remind us of our first Christmas together."

When she would have said something to counter the sentimental thought, he touched a finger to her lips to silence her. "Always," he insisted.

Chapter Fifteen

With the promise of *always* ringing in her ears, Beth sat through their dinner at the inn in a daze. She didn't want to believe in the future. She didn't dare.

And yet Ken seemed so certain. Perhaps he believed enough for both of them.

But as hard as she tried to have faith, she couldn't help remembering how strong Peter's conviction had been, how certain he'd been that Stephanie and Josh would be just fine once they were married, and how terribly, terribly wrong he had turned out to be. How could she ignore her own experience? What would it take to make a believer of her? More than Ken's love, that was clear enough. This time she needed the love of the child, as well. She needed Chelsea's love.

None of them savored the delicious meal. Chelsea was too anxious to finish decorating the tree. She hadn't stopped chattering about the new ornaments since they'd sat down. Ken's attention was focused too completely on Beth. And Beth was lost in her own tumultuous thoughts. They all said no to dessert and were on the way home by seven-thirty.

The phone was ringing as they stepped through the door. "I'll get it," Chelsea said, racing for it.

A moment later a smile of pure delight broke across her face. "Mommy!"

Beth stopped in her tracks, her heart thudding dully in her chest. She tried to tell herself that the child's exuberance was only natural. She reminded herself that she had never intended to replace Pam Hutchinson in Chelsea's heart. She had known all along the folly of trying to fight a child's natural loyalty to a beloved parent. But there was no preventing the unexpected pain that knifed through her.

She glanced at Ken and saw that her dismay was mirrored in his eyes. No doubt he was worried, as she was, about the disruption the call was bound to cause in the insular world they had managed to create for the three of them during these past weeks when Pam had been silent.

"Guess what, Mommy, we're decorating our tree," Chelsea was saying. "Are you going to come to see it? I asked Santa to bring you home. I told him that was the present I wanted more than anything."

Beth swallowed hard against the bitter knot that suddenly seemed to be choking her. There was so much hope in Chelsea's voice, so much love still for the woman who had abandoned her. And that was as it should be, she told herself, as long as Pam didn't dash those hopes so that the healing process had to begin all over again. At seven, Chelsea didn't have the resilience to take another disappointment in stride. In years to come, she might, but not yet. And Chelsea's anguish would ultimately hurt all of them.

But even as Beth watched, Chelsea's face crumpled and her shoulders sagged. "But, Mommy, it's Christmas!" she protested, sounding pitiful. "You have to come. I've made you a present and everything."

Ken sucked in a deep breath and crossed the room, practically snatching the phone from Chelsea's hand. Beth saw the tears gathering in Chelsea's eyes. She knelt down and held out her arms, but Chelsea turned away, leaving her feeling totally bereft and furious with this thoughtless woman whose daughter's needs didn't seem to matter at all.

Not that she had wanted Pam to come to Vermont, she was forced to admit honestly. But for Chelsea's sake, she would have tried to find a way to make it work. Now, putting her own feelings aside, she said, "Chelsea, what did your mommy say?"

"She's not coming."

The reply wasn't unexpected, but Beth felt her heart wrench at Chelsea's obvious distress. What kind of mother would turn her back on her own child at Christmas? she wondered. While she ached to share the joy of waking up on Christmas morning to watch Chelsea's excitement, the woman who had the right to be there refused to come.

"I'm so sorry," she said softly as Ken concluded his hushed exchange with his ex-wife and hung up. "But we'll have a good time. Your daddy's here. Your grandmother's coming and your Uncle Claude and Aunt Harriet. I'll be here."

Chelsea faced her angrily. "I don't want them. I don't want you. I want my mommy," she shouted, and ran upstairs, her feet pounding on the steps as if to emphasize each bitter, hurtful word she'd screamed.

Beth took one step after her, only to have a grim-faced Ken stop her. "I'd better talk to her," he said. He reached out and touched her cheek. "She didn't mean it, you know. She's angry about Pam and taking it out on the rest of us."

"I know," Beth said wearily. She had been through it all before.

Taking off her coat, because she didn't know what else to do, she went into the living room and began unwrapping the new ornaments. She had them all spread out on the carpet when Ken and Chelsea finally came back downstairs. Chelsea's pinched little face was heartbreakingly streaked with tears.

Without even looking at Beth, she methodically picked up the ornaments and put them on the branches. Beth glanced toward Ken, but his thunderous expression didn't invite conversation. She sank back against the pillows on the sofa and felt the wonderful spirit they'd shared earlier in the day slowly evaporate until she had to wonder if it had been real at all. This, she decided bleakly, was reality for a stepfamily.

At last it was time to put the angel on the top of the tree. Chelsea stood in the middle of the floor, the two ornaments side by side in front of her—the traditional one and the brand-new one Ken had bought for

Beth to mark their first Christmas together. Beth wondered which Chelsea would choose, as if that choice carried a significance that went far beyond the mere selection of an adornment for the treetop. She realized she was holding her breath as Chelsea's hand hovered above the two angels. When she reached at last for the glass angel, Beth's breath eased out.

Chelsea picked up the fragile ornament, held it for no longer than a heartbeat, then dropped it with obvious deliberation, not on the carpet, but on the wood floor, where it shattered into hundreds of tiny shards of glass.

"Oh, no," Beth cried, then fell silent as tears stung her eyes.

"Chelsea!" Ken shouted furiously. "Go to your room."

Stunned, Beth stared through her tears at the bits of glass and felt as if they represented the shattered remains of her broken heart. Finally she knelt and began to pick them up. She couldn't bring herself to look at the little girl who hadn't budged despite her father's angry order.

"Chelsea, you heard me," Ken insisted. "Go to your room this instant."

"No. I won't," she said, grabbing the other angel and clutching it tightly. Tears tracked down her forlorn face.

"Why would you do something like this?" he said, sounding more perplexed than furious.

Beth could have told him the answer. Chelsea was holding on to the past in the only way she knew how.

She was rejecting a future that included Beth and not her mother.

As if to confirm it, Chelsea said, "I want this one on the tree. This one is ours. Mommy bought it."

So, Beth thought with a sigh of regret, that was that. Pam would always be there among them. She had known it from the outset, but as recently as a few hours ago she had almost dared to believe they could make it work. The shattered angel proved otherwise.

Holding back her own tears, she stood. "I think I'd better go."

"You don't have your car," Ken protested. "Wait a minute, until we settle this, and I'll take you."

"No," she said sharply. "I'll call Gillie. She'll come."

"Beth, please."

She shook her head. "I'll be fine. Chelsea needs you."

She made the call to Gillie, pulled on her coat and went outside to wait, quietly but ever-so-firmly shutting the door on her dreams.

Ken bit off a curse as he heard the quiet click of the front door. Suddenly he saw all of his plans for marriage going up in smoke. Chelsea was standing in front of him, her whole body shuddering with pent-up sobs. She turned frightened eyes on him.

"I'm sorry, Daddy," she whispered on a broken sob. "I'm sorry. I didn't mean to make Beth go away."

He held out his arms and gathered her close. "I'm sorry, too, baby. I'm sorry, too."

Eventually the storm of tears ended and Chelsea gazed at him sorrowfully. "Is Beth mad at me?"

"What do you think?"

"I'm sorry I broke her angel."

"Why did you?"

"Because I was mad."

"At Beth?"

"No," she said in a small voice. "At Mommy."

"Maybe tomorrow you can call Beth and tell her that."

Chelsea's expression brightened a little. "I have my allowance saved. I could buy her another angel."

He grinned. He knew her piggy bank didn't hold nearly enough to pay for the angel. He also knew that it was incredibly important that she was willing to make the gesture. "I think that might make her very happy."

"Maybe I'll give it to her on Christmas morning."

"Good idea," Ken agreed. He was reassured that Chelsea truly was learning to accept Beth and that this was simply a minor setback. But he wondered how the devil he would ever talk Beth into coming back into their house again. Just this once, he had a feeling his fate might very well be in his daughter's hands.

First thing in the morning, Chelsea brought the portable phone to him and asked him to dial Beth's number. Unfortunately, it rang for quite some time without an answer. Even her answering machine didn't pick up. She had retreated from the world, from them.

"You can try again later," he reassured Chelsea, whose disappointment was no greater than his own.

They spent the morning putting up garlands of evergreen, then went into town to buy another angel, which Chelsea awkwardly wrapped herself and put under the tree. Every hour or so they tried Beth again, all to no avail. Ken had a hunch she had the phone unplugged and the answering machine turned off deliberately.

It was late afternoon when the brainstorm hit him. He made a couple of calls, made a thermos of hot chocolate, tucked the engagement ring he'd bought a few days earlier into his pocket and bundled up Chelsea. He'd been thinking for weeks that Christmas would be the perfect time to propose, but somehow tonight seemed right.

"Where are we going, Daddy?"

"You'll see."

By the time they reached Roger Killington's, the bank president had hitched a team of horses to the restored sleigh that Ken had asked to store in his barn.

"Perfect night for a sleigh ride," Roger said. "You going to pick up Beth?"

"I'm going to try," Ken said.

Roger laughed at his grim tone. "Good luck."

"Believe me, I'll need it."

Chelsea was so excited about riding in the sleigh, it was all he could do to keep her seated beside him. They glided across the snow, following a stream of moonlight. The bells on the reins jingled a merry tune that had him grinning with anticipation. This had to charm the socks right off her. What woman could resist a romantic sleigh ride that was capped off with a proposal?

Apparently Beth had heard the bells—or else Roger had called to warn her—because she was waiting on her front porch when they pulled up outside.

"Go tell her you're sorry," Ken whispered to Chelsea. "She won't come with us unless you do."

Chelsea shot him a frightened look, but with an incredible display of pint-size bravado she slid down and scampered off across the snow. Ken couldn't hear what she said, but Beth knelt down and pulled her into a tight hug. He considered that a good sign. The best, in fact.

He walked over to join them. "Care to go for a sleigh ride with us? You promised, remember?"

Beth's gaze shifted from Chelsea to him, then moved on to the sleigh. "Is that the one you bought at the auction?" she inquired, amazement written all over her face.

"That's the one. Isn't it a beauty?"

Taking Chelsea's hand, she crossed over to the sleigh. The man Beth had hired to do the restoration had done it exactly as he'd envisioned. The runners glistened. The sleigh was shiny with new paint and gold trim. The seats had been upholstered with soft black leather. A bright red wool blanket was draped across the wide seat.

"I never would have believed it," Beth said. "It's like something from a Christmas card."

"A Currier and Ives print," he agreed.

"And Mr. Killington loaned us the horses," Chelsea chimed in. "They're gray. He says I can come over and he'll teach me to ride sometime. You know what else? He has cows. He showed them to me. And he says he has a granddaughter who's just my age. She's going to come for Christmas.''

"That's right," Beth said. "Her name is Melanie. I think you'll really like her.''

Chelsea's expression sobered. "Do you think she'd be my friend? I don't have any friends here yet, not like at home. My friends there came over to play. Here it's too far.''

"I think she would love to be your friend. And my friend Gillie has a little girl who's in your class at school. Her name is Jessie.''

Chelsea's expression brightened. "I know Jessie. She's really fun. You know her?''

"Very well. Maybe you could have a tea party for them on Christmas day when your daddy has his open house.''

Chelsea's eyes widened as she looked up at him hopefully. "Can I, Daddy?''

"If Beth will help you. I'm afraid I don't know much about tea parties.''

"Will you, Beth? Will you? We could have little sandwiches and cookies and ice cream and candy.''

Ken gave an exaggerated groan, but his gaze was locked on Beth. Chelsea's request seemed to have gotten around her defenses again. Trying to keep the mood light, he said, "Dear Heaven, and I don't even know the dentist in town yet.''

Beth grinned at him. "You will. In the meantime, Chelsea and I will try to come up with a slightly less sugary menu.''

"Does that mean you'll help?" Chelsea demanded.

There was an instant's hesitation that had Ken holding his breath, then she nodded. "I would love to help," she agreed.

"Good, then that's settled," Ken said in a rush to conclude the deal before she could change her mind. "Now button up that coat and climb aboard. I can't wait to try this thing out and see if it's as romantic as I figured it would be."

He pinned his gaze on Beth as he said it and watched the color rise in her cheeks. He held out his hand to help her into the sleigh. Chelsea had already managed to climb in and was settled in the middle of the seat. He frowned at her. "Over, little one."

"But I want to sit next to you and Beth."

He caught Beth's grin and realized that his scheme had just gone up in smoke. So much for romance. Chelsea probably held the key to his capturing Beth's heart and holding it, anyway.

When his two ladies were settled, he took the reins in hand and guided the horses toward the open field behind Beth's house. For the next two hours they glided across the moonlit landscape, drinking hot chocolate and once again fracturing a long list of carols with their off-key voices and improvised words.

"If we don't get inside soon, our frostbite will be decidedly unromantic," Beth finally warned, her cheeks rosy and her eyes sparkling.

She looked, Ken thought, radiant. More, she appeared to be contented. If nothing else, this outing had washed away the shadows caused by Chelsea's behavior the day before.

"Come with me to drop the sleigh off and I'll drive you home afterward, okay?" he suggested, thinking of the diamond ring that was practically burning a hole in his pocket.

She nodded.

Ken slid his arm across his sleepy daughter and captured Beth's gloved hand in his own. "Thank you for coming tonight."

"I wouldn't have missed it."

A few minutes later as they returned to Roger's, he came out in the yard to greet them. At the sight of Beth, the older man grinned. "I see he talked you into going out. The man might make a New Englander yet. Doesn't seem to care that the temperature's heading for zero and more snow's expected any minute now."

Ken plucked a couple of foot warmers from the floor of the sleigh, along with the now-empty thermos. "The key is preparation."

Roger laughed. "I'd say the warmers and the hot chocolate didn't have much to do with it. I'd say there's more heat in the way you two look at each other."

Ken watched Beth's face flame and laughed along with Roger. "There's some truth to that," he said, starting to lead the horses back to the barn.

"I'll take them," Roger offered. "You run along. Your girl there looks as if she's asleep on her feet and I think you and Beth have better things to do than stabling my horses."

Again, Ken's thoughts went to the ring in his pocket. "Just this once," he agreed.

"Merry Christmas," Roger called after them as they made their way to the car.

"Merry Christmas!" Ken called back. "We'll see you on Christmas afternoon. Chelsea's anxious to meet your granddaughter, so be sure to bring her along."

"Right, son. You drive carefully."

Turning onto the road a few minutes later, Ken headed toward his house. Beth glanced over at him. "I thought you were taking me home first."

"Chelsea needs to get to bed."

"But once she's there, you can't leave to take me home."

He kept his gaze level. "I know," he said quietly. "Stay tonight."

"Ken..." she began, but the protest never went any further.

"If you really insist, I'll turn around," he offered.

"I suppose...I suppose it will be okay," she said. Suddenly she grinned. "After all, there are plenty of bedrooms there. I should know. I decorated every one of them."

"You won't be staying in a guest room," he countered.

She settled back against the seat of the car, a half smile on her lips. "We'll see," she said. "A man should never get too sure of himself."

The deliberate taunt stirred his blood. "You should never challenge a desperate man."

She faced him, her expression all innocence. "Why is that?"

"It just makes us all the more determined to get our way."

"How fascinating," she said. "I can hardly wait to see you try."

If Chelsea hadn't been in the car, Ken would have started trying right then and there. He knew for a fact how quickly he could make Beth's pulse race, how easily he could set off a trembling that scrambled through her entire body. The more she resisted, the more fun it was to sneak past her defenses.

He sent her a look that he hoped spoke volumes about his intentions. Her response was a sassy grin that made his entire body tighten with need. Right now, he figured it was a toss-up which one of them was better at the game he'd foolishly initiated.

He carried Chelsea inside and headed up the stairs with her. At the top, she woke up. "Are we home?"

"Yep. Change into your nightgown and hop into bed."

"But I haven't had my bath," she protested sleepily.

"You don't need one tonight."

"But I always take a bath before I go to bed."

Ken thought of the woman waiting downstairs for him. "Just this once, your bath can wait until morning," he assured Chelsea. "Come on. Into your nightgown and into bed."

"Is Beth here?"

"She's downstairs."

"I want her to read me a story."

Ken barely contained a groan. "Sweetie, you'll be asleep before she reads the first paragraph."

"I always have a bedtime story, Daddy. You know that," she insisted stubbornly.

Sighing deeply, he finally relented, mainly because he knew Beth would be pleased by the request. "I'll get her, but you'd better be all tucked in when I get back."

"Okay."

He called to Beth from the top of the stairs. When she appeared in the foyer below, he said, "Chelsea wants you to read her a bedtime story."

A smile of absolute pleasure spread across her face. She looked so delighted, Ken was glad he'd broken down and asked. She practically took the steps two at a time, though it was clear she was trying to contain her enthusiasm.

"What book does she want me to read? Does she have a favorite?" She looked up at him worriedly. "What if I'm no good at this?"

"Didn't you ever read to your stepchildren?"

"They were too old."

"Well, take it from me, the technique is less important than just showing up. Chelsea loves this ritual. I couldn't talk her out of it."

"I'm glad you didn't," Beth admitted.

Inside Chelsea's room, he stood back and watched as Beth and his daughter chose a book from the dozens on Chelsea's shelves.

"*Little Women,*" Beth said, rubbing her hand over the embossed binding. "Oh, how I loved this when I was a little girl."

"You've read it?" Chelsea asked, her astonishment plain.

"Over and over," Beth admitted.

"Will you read it to me? All of it?"

"It's a big book and you're very sleepy."

"We don't have to finish tonight. You could read it to me every night," Chelsea said, yawning as she scrambled under the covers.

Beth pulled them up under her chin, then settled into the chair beside the bed and began to read. As Ken had anticipated, her voice quickly lulled Chelsea to sleep, but still she read on as if just being there brought her joy. He couldn't bring himself to cut her off.

Finally, when the chapter ended, she closed the book and glanced his way. Putting the book aside, she leaned down and kissed Chelsea's cheek and smoothed her hair away from her face. "Sleep well," she whispered, then joined Ken in the hallway.

"I told you you'd do fine," he said. "You made her very happy."

"Not nearly as happy as she made me. If only..." Her voice trailed off.

"Stop that," he told her, silencing her with a kiss. "*If only* is a very sad phrase. There are only certainties in our future."

She smiled, but there was no mistaking the regret in her eyes. "If only..." she began, mocking him. "If only that were true."

"We can make it true," he told her, leading her into the living room where the lights twinkling on the tree provided the only illumination. When she was curled up at the end of the sofa, he settled himself beside her and drew in a deep breath. Her suddenly wary expression wasn't helping matters.

"Beth, you know how I feel about you," he began.

"Ken, don't," she whispered, touching a finger to his lips. "It won't work and you know it."

"No," he insisted, taking her hand, brushing a kiss across the knuckles, then holding it tightly. "Listen to me, please. If I haven't told you in words how much I love you, then I hope you've seen it in the way I am when I'm with you. I'm at peace with myself and, believe me, contentment is something I never expected to find when I moved here. You make me want to look ahead, not back."

He looked into her dismayed eyes and nearly stopped. Instead he hurried on. "You would make me extremely happy if you would agree to become my wife." He pulled the velvet box from his pocket, flipped it open to reveal a stunning diamond and held it out.

She didn't take it. She barely even looked at it. Suddenly his heart seemed to still and then outright panic set in. She was going to turn him down, he realized as his heart thudded dully in his chest.

Finally she glanced at the ring, then at the precariously tilting angel on the top of the Christmas tree. Pam's angel. Her expression filled with dismay and Ken cursed his decision to propose to her in the very room where Chelsea had so recently rejected her.

He studied her face and wished he had done things differently. Gazing at last directly into her troubled eyes, he thought he saw longing. Longing and dread.

In that moment he realized that the dread would win. All of her doubts hadn't been erased. Even a blind man should have been able to tell that. Even a fool would have had sense enough to wait. He also saw now that no matter how much she loved him, no matter how much she loved Chelsea, she would never agree to marry him until his daughter gave them her wholehearted blessing, as well.

That fragile glass angel, too recently shattered, stood between them as staunchly as a wall made of stone.

Chapter Sixteen

Ken was at a loss. How was he going to convince Beth that Chelsea would be happy about their marriage? She would never just take his word for it. She might not even take Chelsea's word. It might require more solid proof, more bedtime stories, more spontaneous, similarly trusting gestures on his daughter's part. In time those would add up, but Ken was impatient. He desperately wanted to find a way to prod things along.

He sat downstairs long after Beth had gone up to sleep in one of the guest rooms, alone, refusing to even consider his company beneath the pile of down comforters. He considered a dozen schemes to charm or seduce her, then dismissed them. It was past time for schemes, charm or seduction. Only honesty and straightforward actions would accomplish the results he wanted.

Ken thought he knew how Chelsea had come to feel about Beth, but it was clear that Beth didn't trust her own assessment of the child's feelings. An image of that shattered angel came back to haunt him.

And then he was struck by the realization that a replacement, bought with nickels and dimes and a little parental monetary assistance, and wrapped with loving if inept hands, was sitting right under the tree. Would it be enough? Would that send a message to Beth as nothing else had?

Finally, a plan beginning to form in his mind, he climbed the stairs. Hesitating outside the door to the guest room, he sighed and moved on to the beautifully decorated but incredibly lonely master suite. Despite what she thought when she chose the room down the hall, he knew that Beth would be in that king-size bed with him tonight. He would feel her presence, ache for her, as if she were physically right beside him.

Sure enough, no sooner had his head hit the pillow than his imagination went wild. He pictured her pale skin touched by moonlight, the tips of her breasts hardening beneath his touch, her legs wrapping around him as her hips rose to meet his. His body throbbed under the vivid spell she had cast over his senses.

''Damn,'' he muttered, cursing her for a passionate witch.

He could see her laughing at the curse, taunting him to come closer, closer, and then holding him at bay. He moaned and buried his head under a pillow, as if that would keep out the images.

It didn't. He was still tossing and turning, tormented by a restless, unfulfilled longing when dawn broke on what he knew was going to be the most important day of his entire life.

Beth slipped downstairs on the morning following Ken's proposal and made yet another desperation call to Gillie.

"This is getting to be a habit," her friend said fifteen minutes later when she had pulled up in front of the house and Beth was in the car. "I wonder if I should charge taxi rates."

"You owe me," Beth reminded her curtly. "I would never have gotten involved with the man in the first place, if you hadn't neglected to tell me that Ken had a daughter."

"I know. I thought once the two of you got to know each other it really wouldn't matter. I figured the kind of disaster you'd been through with Peter couldn't possibly happen a second time." Gillie regarded her with obvious regret. "I'm sorry. How many times do I have to tell you that?"

"I'll let you know when you can stop," Beth said dryly.

Gillie glanced away, but not before Beth caught her smile.

"Are we going for coffee?" Gillie asked.

"Might as well, unless you have to get home to take the kids to school."

"Daniel said he'd get them there this morning." She glanced at Beth. "Would it be considered extremely indelicate of me to point out that a woman sneaking out of a man's house at dawn does not seem like a woman who's protesting too much over the state of their affair?"

"There is no affair," Beth said bleakly. "Not anymore, anyway."

"But you stayed there last night."

"In a guest room."

Gillie shook her head as if to clear it. "Maybe this better wait until I have coffee."

Beth scowled at her. "I can almost guarantee it won't make any more sense then."

"Let's just see about that," Gillie said, pulling into a space in front of Lou's bakery. "Not another word until I have caffeine pumping through my veins."

Beth would have let the conversation lag a whole lot longer than that, but the instant her friend had her coffee and a heavily frosted cinnamon bun, Gillie said, "Okay, what's going on?"

Beth gave her the short version, which included only the call from Pam, the deliberately shattered angel, and Ken's proposal.

"I see," Gillie said slowly. She shook her head. "No, I don't see, at all. He loves you. He proposed to you. Chelsea apologized. What do you want? If you're waiting for a guarantee carved in stone that nothing like this will ever happen again, forget it. It will. Kids fling hateful words at their birth parents, too, whenever things don't suit them."

Beth regarded her with skepticism. "Jessie and Daniel Jr. have never said they hated you."

"Jessie told me just last week she hated me and would never speak to me again," Gillie countered.

"Why?" Beth asked, shocked.

"Because I wouldn't let her wear her shorts and a T-shirt to school. She didn't want to hear that it was below freezing outside."

Beth waved it off. "But that's just plain silly. Of course she didn't mean it."

"At the time she meant it. And when she said it, it hurt," Gillie admitted. "But over the course of a lifetime, it was an insignificant, meaningless bit of rebellion. I suspect I'll hear it again and again, especially when she wants to date, wear makeup and take the car."

"What about Daniel Jr.?" Beth asked. The preschooler was the most placid child she'd ever seen. She couldn't imagine him getting riled up enough to hate anything. He'd never even splattered his baby food in protest over the abominable taste.

"We exchanged several heated words during potty training," Gillie said, grinning at her.

Beth sighed. "You think I'm making too much out of all this."

"No. Given your past, I'd say you are being sensibly cautious." Her gaze turned serious. "Do you love him?"

"Yes."

"Do you love Chelsea?"

Beth grinned ruefully. "Most of the time."

"Will giving them up now hurt any less than giving them up if it doesn't work out?"

"Probably not," she admitted.

"Nothing of value in this life comes without risks," Gillie observed. "You could wait around for some bachelor who's never been married, who doesn't have kids, and then discover that he's still tied to Mama's apron strings. It's hard to find anyone our age who doesn't come without some sort of emotional baggage. You included, I might point out. Ken knows what you've been through. Isn't he making a real effort to prove that it won't be the same this time? Isn't he disciplining Chelsea? Hasn't he done everything in his power to build the bond between the two of you?"

Beth thought of all the engineered meetings, of all the space he'd given to her and Chelsea, putting his own desires on a back burner for the sake of a long-term relationship. "He's been wonderful," she admitted.

"Not like Peter?"

"Nothing at all like Peter," she agreed, and suddenly she could feel hope blossoming again. Ken was infinitely wiser than Peter. He had the patience to mediate, the strength to discipline, the determination to find answers rather than to place blame. She smiled as relief and a sudden buoyant optimism sighed through her. "Thank you."

"Does that mean I should start dieting so I can fit into a dress suitable for a fancy wedding?"

Beth shook her head. "Start looking for one you can wear as matron of honor."

* * *

Right up until Christmas Eve, Ken worked on his plan. He'd been dismayed when he'd realized that Beth had slipped out of the house the morning after his proposal, but then he'd decided it was for the best. It would give him time to do it right the next time. He wanted the time, the setting, everything working in his favor. What could be better than Christmas morning?

He waited until he and Chelsea were exiting Christmas Eve services to approach Beth. The smile she turned on him was just a little uncertain and yet there was an unmistakable air of serenity about her. He wondered what that was all about. He could only pray that it would prove beneficial for achieving his goal.

"Merry Christmas," he said quietly.

"Merry Christmas."

"Guess what?" Chelsea chimed in. "Santa Claus is coming tonight." A worried frown suddenly puckered her brow. "He wouldn't come while we're not there, would he, Daddy?"

"Nope. He makes his rounds in the middle of the night, when good little boys and girls are sound asleep."

Chelsea reached for his hand and tugged. "Then let's hurry. I want to go to sleep, so Santa can come."

"In just a minute. I need to ask Beth something." He turned back to her. "Will you join us in the morning? We would really like you there when we open presents."

"Please come," Chelsea chimed in.

Ken was grateful for the spontaneous accord. He knew the invitation would be more likely to be successful if it clearly came from both of them.

Beth's eyes sparkled. "I would love to. What time?"

"The earlier the better. I'm not sure how long after dawn I can contain Chelsea."

"Then I'll be there at dawn," she agreed.

As she walked away, Ken uttered a sigh of relief. So far, so good. He wasn't about to kid himself, though. The hardest part was yet to come.

On Christmas morning Ken had coffee perking by 6:00 a.m. This was one year when his impatience outpaced Chelsea's. He'd already showered and dressed. He'd turned on the tree lights, built a fire, and turned the stereo on low, filling the downstairs with carols.

Every five minutes he paced to the bottom of the stairs to listen for Chelsea, then walked back to the window to peer out into the darkness, hoping to see Beth's car. He wanted Chelsea downstairs first, all dressed and ready for their guest. In another five minutes, he'd go up and wake her, he decided.

Fortunately, excitement and the softly playing music did the trick. Chelsea appeared at the top of the stairs. "Daddy, did Santa come?" she asked sleepily.

Ken met her halfway up the stairs. "He certainly did. Why don't you put on some clothes, so you'll look really pretty when Beth gets here? Then we can see what Santa left."

Within minutes, Chelsea was racing down the stairs in a new dress and her best patent leather shoes. Just as they reached the living room, where piles of presents waited beneath the tree, he heard Beth's car drive up, then the sound of her footsteps crunching through the snow. He knew that at any second she would walk through the front door.

Silently mouthing a heartfelt prayer that he could pull this off, he placed the engagement ring on the coffee table in front of Chelsea. His daughter regarded it with a frown creasing her brow.

"What's that?"

"An engagement ring."

"For Beth?"

He heard Beth's footsteps come to a halt just inside the front door, which he'd left ajar for her. "Actually Beth turned it down," he said loudly enough to be heard by anyone who happened to be eavesdropping.

Chelsea's eyes widened. A satisfying expression of disbelief spread across her face. "She doesn't want to marry you? Why not?"

"I think she's worried about how you'll feel about having her as a stepmother," he said bluntly. It was a calculated risk. He'd learned the hard way that Chelsea could be unpredictable. But he also believed with all his heart that she adored Beth as much as he did. And an uncensored response was the only kind Beth would ever trust. He waited, his breath caught in his throat.

To his astonishment, Chelsea climbed down from the sofa and walked into the foyer. Ken followed and saw her facing down the woman in question, hands on tiny hips. Her whole body was practically quivering with indignation.

"Is it true?" she demanded.

"Is what true?" Beth asked with amazing aplomb for a woman being cross-examined by a pint-size interrogator who could hold the key to her future.

"That you don't want to marry my daddy?"

Beth's gaze came up and met his. "That's not what I said."

"Will you or won't you?" Chelsea demanded impatiently. "He's a great daddy."

"Thanks for the vote of confidence, Shortstuff," Ken said, his gaze locked with Beth's. "So, what's it going to be?"

Beth looked from him to Chelsea and back again. Then she hunkered down in front of the child. "Are you proposing to me on your father's behalf, or is this what you want, too?"

Chelsea considered the question thoughtfully, while Ken held his breath. His daughter's answer was going to make all the difference in how this unorthodox proposal turned out.

"You don't yell at me much," Chelsea conceded. "And you picked out a great Christmas tree." Her gaze narrowed. "Will you ever punish me?"

"Only if you're bad."

"Oh," Chelsea said, then seemed to accept the honest answer. "Can you bake chocolate-chip cookies?"

"They're my favorite," Beth admitted, rising to stand beside Ken.

Chelsea nodded. "Then I guess you'd make an okay stepmom."

"Is that a yes?" Ken inquired hopefully, looking from one to the other.

"Yes," his daughter said, and held out the ring to Beth. "Want it?"

So much for flowery words, Ken thought ruefully. Beth's reply was so long in coming and so softly spoken that at first he wasn't sure he'd heard her.

"Was that a yes?" he asked.

She knelt down and took Chelsea's hands in her own. "Are you sure?"

Chelsea nodded and Beth's gaze rose to meet his. "Then the answer is definitely yes. Yes, I will marry you."

"All right!" Chelsea whooped. "Can we bake cookies right after we open Christmas presents?"

"We can bake them every day for the next month," Ken said as he drew Beth and then his daughter into his arms. "First, though, don't you have a present you'd like to give Beth?"

"Oh, yeah," Chelsea said, running ahead of them into the living room and plucking the awkwardly wrapped gift from the pile under the tree. "This is for you from me."

There was a glow in Beth's eyes that Ken could have sworn he'd never seen before.

"I wonder what this could be?" Beth said, shaking the box gently as Chelsea watched worriedly.

"Open it."

Beth undid the ribbon with slow deliberation, almost as if she couldn't quite bear to have this special moment end. She was just as cautious as she slipped off the paper.

Chelsea rested her hands on Beth's knees and watched her intently. "Hurry," she urged.

When Beth finally lifted the lid from the box and saw the angel cushioned in its nest of tissue paper, tears welled up in her eyes and spilled down her cheeks.

Chelsea regarded her with dismay. "Don't you like it? It's just like the one I broke."

Shaking her head, Beth gathered the child into her arms. "No, it's not," she said gently. "This one is truly special."

"Why?" Chelsea asked.

"Because it came from you." She tilted her head until her gaze met Ken's. "I love you. Both of you."

Ken swallowed hard against the emotion clogging his throat. Before he could find the words to express how it felt to share Christmas morning with the woman he loved and the daughter he adored, Chelsea broke free of Beth's embrace and raced back to the tree. She stood there staring indecisively at all the presents, then turned back to Beth.

"I think you're the very best present I'm going to get this year."

"Oh, baby," Beth whispered. "You are definitely the very best present I'm getting." She glanced up at Ken and smiled. "And you, of course."

He sighed. Upstaged by his daughter again. "Of course," he said, then leaned down to kiss his bride-to-be. This, however, was one area where he definitely had the edge.

* * * * *

MONTANA™
Mavericks

Stories that capture living and loving beneath the Big Sky, where legends live on...and mystery lingers.

This December, explore more MONTANA MAVERICKS with

THE RANCHER TAKES A WIFE
by Jackie Merritt

He'd made up his mind. He'd loved her almost a lifetime and now he was going to have her, come hell or high water.

And don't miss a minute of the loving as the passion continues with:

OUTLAW LOVERS
by Pat Warren (January)

WAY OF THE WOLF
by Rebecca Daniels (February)

THE LAW IS NO LADY
by Helen R. Myers (March)
and many more!

Only from *Silhouette*® where passion lives.

HUSBAND: SOME ASSEMBLY REQUIRED
Marie Ferrarella
(SE #931, January)

Murphy Pendleton's act of bravery landed him in the hospital—and right back in Shawna Saunders's life. She'd lost her heart to him before—and now this dashing real-life hero was just too tempting to resist. He could be the Mr. Right Shawna was waiting for....

Don't miss
HUSBAND: SOME ASSEMBLY REQUIRED,
by Marie Ferrarella,
available in January!

She's friend, wife, mother—she's you! And beside each Special Woman stands a wonderfully *special* man. It's a celebration of our heroines— and the men who become part of their lives.

Silhouette
SPECIAL EDITION™

WHAT EVER HAPPENED TO...?

Have you been wondering when much-loved characters will finally get their own stories? Well, have we got a lineup for you! Silhouette Special Edition is proud to present a *Spin-off Spectacular!* Be sure to catch these exciting titles from some of your favorite authors:

HUSBAND: SOME ASSEMBLY REQUIRED (SE #931 January) Shawna Saunders has finally found Mr. Right in the dashing Murphy Pendleton, last seen in *Marie Ferrarella*'s BABY IN THE MIDDLE (SE #892).

SAME TIME, NEXT YEAR (SE #937 February) In this tie-in to *Debbie Macomber*'s popular series THOSE MANNING MEN and THOSE MANNING SISTERS, a yearly reunion between friends suddenly has them in the marrying mood!

A FAMILY HOME (SE #938 February) Adam Cutler discovers the best reason for staying home is the love he's found with sweet-natured and sexy Lainey Bates in *Celeste Hamilton*'s follow-up to WHICH WAY IS HOME? (SE #897).

JAKE'S MOUNTAIN (SE #945 March) Jake Harris never met anyone as stubborn—or as alluring—as Dr. Maggie Matthews in *Christine Flynn*'s latest, a spin-off to WHEN MORNING COMES (SE #922).

Don't miss these wonderful titles, only for our readers—only from Silhouette Special Edition!

Silhouette SPECIAL EDITION ™

Open the latest of Lisa Jackson's...

Love Letters

C IS FOR COWBOY (December, SE #926)

Mysterious forces stalked Casey McKee's powerful family, suddenly making her a target. Only brooding cowboy Sloan Redhawk could save her—and only Casey could make this loner's passion stir anew!

And, in the fall of 1995, be sure to catch the next book in the series—

D IS FOR DESTINY

Dani Donahue had only one wish in life: to find the son she gave up for adoption. But she never imagined her search would bring her back into the arms of Brandon Scarlotti, the father of her child, and the man who was her destiny....

**Don't miss any of Lisa Jackson's
LOVE LETTERS— Sometimes all it takes is a letter of love to rebuild dreams of the past....**

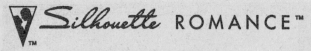

Also available by popular author

SHERRYL WOODS

Silhouette Special Edition®